THE BRANDIRON SERIES

THE TEXAS BADGE

DUSTY RICHARDS

WHEELER PUBLISHING
A part of Gale, a Cengage Company

 GALE
A Cengage Company

Farmington Hills, Mich • San Francisco • New York • Waterville, Maine
Meriden, Conn • Mason, Ohio • Chicago

Copyright © 2016 by Dusty Richards.
The Brandiron Series.
Wheeler Publishing, a part of Gale, a Cengage Company.

ALL RIGHTS RESERVED
The characters and events in this book are fictitious. Any similarity to real persons, living or dead, is entirely coincidental and not intended by the author.
Wheeler Publishing Large Print Western.
The text of this Large Print edition is unabridged.
Other aspects of the book may vary from the original edition.
Set in 16 pt. Plantin.

LIBRARY OF CONGRESS CIP DATA ON FILE.
CATALOGUING IN PUBLICATION FOR THIS BOOK
IS AVAILABLE FROM THE LIBRARY OF CONGRESS

ISBN-13: 978-1-4328-4964-1 (softcover)

Published in 2018 by arrangement with Galway Press, an imprint of Oghma Creative Media

Printed in the United States of America
2 3 4 5 6   23 22 21 20 19

THE TEXAS BADGE

Date: 11/4/19

LP FIC RICHARDS
Richards, Dusty
The Texas badge

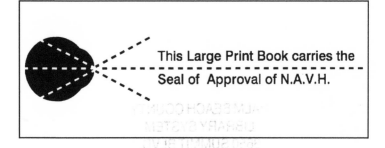

This Large Print Book carries the
Seal of Approval of N.A.V.H.

For Mike Miller

FOREWORD

The idea for this book came to me in a dream. I woke one night and someone was hollering for the sheriff, so I got up and wrote it down. Then things began to happen on paper — I met the woman in this new hero's life, measured him up some, and the rest here waiting for you to turn the pages and discover it yourself. Some books roll out like that, like a bedroll untied. Others you fret over, making plot shifts that end up in blind canyons. Those kind keep you awake at night when the words won't come to deliver you from your plight in the waking hours looking at an un-filled screen. Then, snail-like, it works its way through the writing process and you finally have a finished book in your hands, ready for the judgement of your publisher. Thankfully, mine, though small, is one of the best.

Master craftsman Casey Cowan and his crew at Oghma Creative Media work hard to wrap up a better-than-plain copy of my words, and even let me pick some of the cover setup.

Gil Miller, who as an FFA member ran the tie down event chutes at his Chapter's Junior Rodeo that I announced many years ago, is my able editor. We laughed over that one night about our first meeting. Gil came to my writer's group to learn the ropes as a beginning writer, but has since become the master, and I couldn't be happier. Joined by the likes of a few other up-and-coming authors and editors like Gordon Bonnet, Prix Gautney, and Staci Troilo, they turned my rough draft into the polished work you now hold in your hands — all while writing novels of their own. Look up their names, and you'll find some damn great books in their own right.

Thanks also to Sophia Murray, who helps run my digital media, and photographer Kelly D. Willis, who spent hours in an Oklahoma pasture taking photos from every angle trying to find one that actually made me look good.

Even with help, though, this book-writing business has been and still is lots of headaches, crossed eyes, and laughter. You can't blame the computer for mistakes, because the operator on the keys, not the machine, makes most of them. You write a book and wonder what you left out — edit it ten times and still find typos. They pop up like prairie dogs. New one shows up every time. But, God willing, The Brandiron rides on to more western adventures and awakenings in the night.

Thanks for taking the time to read with me. Feel free to drop me a line anytime at dustyrichards@cox.net. I love hearing from my fans, and I'll always reply.

— *Dusty Richards*
February 5, 2016
Springdale, Arkansas

ONE

"Sheriff Dell Hoffman. Sheriff Dell Hoffman?" Someone out in front of the house was yelling at him. What time was it? Still night. His finger silenced the waking naked woman sharing his bed.

"Stay. They don't know you're here. I have no idea whatever is wrong." He rose, put on his shirt, then slipped the Colt out of its holster on the wall peg. At the upstairs bedroom window he raised the bottom half with his left hand and the other fist held his six-gun at his side, ready in case this was some kind of a trap.

"What in the hell is wrong?"

"They've robbed the bank."

"Is Marshal Hanks down there?"

"Yes, he's down there. He sent me to get you. Arnold Thompson was murdered and Hanks told me to get you."

"Thompson was murdered?" she whispered, clutching the sheet to cover her nakedness.

"He must be. Stay put. I'll go see about it." He raised his voice to shout at the man at his front yard gate. "Go back and help him. I'll be along quick as I can get dressed."

"I'll do it, Sheriff. He said he sure needed you."

"Good. I'm coming." He closed the window and buttoned his shirt. What else was wrong?

She sat up on the edge of bed and reached for her slip. "Nothing like you being the only law in town, is there?" On her feet, she wiggled the slip down over her tall, slender body. "Don't apologize. I know you didn't plan it. But who murdered the banker? That sounds tough. Why kill him?"

He pulled on his pants and whispered, "I have no answer, Guinn. But I'll soon know more."

She came over and hugged him. "Sorry. I know. It's only a small interruption."

They kissed and he held her to him. "I'll make it up. Can you make it home all right?"

"No problem. I can slip back and forth between here and my sister Nan's house and no one will notice. You be careful. Let me know when the coast is clear." She kissed his cheek.

"You know I'll do that." He unbuckled his gun belt and cinched it around his waist, then put it back, reset the holster.

"Dell, be careful. I really enjoyed our short evening with each other."

"Me, too, sweetheart."

"I'll be here for you when you have time. You know that."

"Be careful. The whole town may be awake."

"No problem." She stood on her toes and kissed him again on the cheek. "Take care of your business."

He put on his hat and hurried out the bedroom door and down the stairs. When he came off the porch, it was plain the word was out. Through the night, hastily dressed people headed up the dirt street for the town's two blocks of businesses.

"That you, Sheriff? You hear about the robbery?"

"I just got woke up and learned about it. I'm on my way there now."

"My banker dead?"

"I don't know. I will shortly. If he is, we'll sure get the men who did it."

"Sheriff, I believe you will. Sure be a sad day tomorrow if he is dead."

"You're right about that." Dell took off at a run, Guinn's perfume still in his nose. The scent reminded him of his pleasures with her earlier. Shame they couldn't have slept — they'd even planned to have breakfast leisurely at his house in the morning.

There was a crowd outside the bank, and he excused his way through them. His jailer, Guy Branch, held them back at the door.

"All well at the jail?" he asked his man.

"Fine. Cells are all locked, and so is the front door. I hurried down here to help Hanks. It sure ain't nice in there but he's preserving the murder scene."

"I think you need to get someone to take your place here. There are some dangerous criminals involved in this crime, and they may have more plans than a robbery."

"I can do that. I just —"

"You did the right thing to do this, Guy. Marshal Hanks needed you. I'm simply concerned. We need to be sure we cover the jail."

"I'll get someone for here. Sorry —"

"No, we are all in an uproar and you were right. Has anyone sent for Deputy Caine?"

"Yes sir. I had a boy ride a horse for his place."

"Good. You pick a man to take your place here. May be nothing, but I try to follow my inclinations."

Dell went inside the well-lighted bank.

The dead banker lay face down on the floor. His bloody white shirt looked like they gave him two fatal buckshot wounds in his back at point blank range.

Pained-faced, hatless town marshal Fred Hanks rose from the swivel chair. "Glad you got here, Dell. I was two blocks away at Niles Livery when all hell broke loose down here. I had been by here maybe twenty minutes earlier. Nothing was happening. But when I heard the shotgun blast I started up here. Four or five horsemen charged off in the night. They must have forced him to come down here and open the safe. They cleaned all the money out of the open safe, and went charging off to the east."

"Anyone go tell his wife yet?" Dell asked.

"No sir."

"I'm going to his house and tell her. Keep this room preserved."

"I'll do that."

Several joined him as he hurried for the Arnold Thompson house. En route, the people asked questions he answered only with short replies that amounted to, "We will see."

The house was dark and he tried the door. "Missus Thompson?"

No reply. She had to be in there.

He busted open the front door with his

shoulder. With his hands to show them to stay back he told the curious, "Everyone stay back."

Once inside he found a lamp on a table, lighted it, and looked around. Nothing appeared out of place downstairs. He took the stairs two at a time.

In the first bedroom he discovered Janet Thompson sprawled naked on the bed with her throat cut. He swallowed down the sour bile behind his tongue, then went down the hall. There the three children lay dead. The younger boys had been brutally murdered with their hands tied behind their back. Their teenage daughter, Wendy, was naked. She'd been ravaged, then killed in the same fashion as her mother.

In shock, Dell backed to the door.

What kind of devils would do this sort of thing to innocent victims? No doubt they'd taken Thompson prisoner here in his house, threatening harm to his family unless he took them to the bank and opened the safe. Then while he was gone, the ones left behind had raped and killed the whole bunch.

It was without doubt the most horrible scene he could ever remember in all his years of law enforcement.

He told those crowding in the front door

to get outside the house. "This is a murder scene and needs to be examined."

"They dead?" someone asked.

He had them all outside the house and held his hands up to quiet them. "This is the worst crime scene I have ever seen in my life. All of them have been murdered."

A horse and rider showed up and his deputy, Wilbur Caine, came through the crowd. "All the prisoners have been turned out of the jail, Dell."

"The Cody boys, too?" The two brothers were waiting in the jail to be hung. This bunch of killers had his small force spread out over the robbery — no doubt the fact he came to help Hanks saved his jailer's life.

Damn. These bastards aren't even human.

"Them and the rest of the prisoners," Wilbur said.

"The robbery was a cover up, wasn't it?" he asked his man.

"Must have been, Dell. Sorry, I came when the boy woke me."

"We couldn't have stopped it. They knew our every move. I was sound asleep." He shook his head, then sat down on the top porch step and mopped his face. All the death, blood, and destruction shocked him, happening in the small town where he was responsible for their safety. The episode

17

stabbed him like a knife deep in his chest and brain as well.

When he spoke to Wilbur he said, "I need two men to guard this house until the three of us can examine the entire thing. I'm going back to the bank. We'll need some armed men to gather up all the prisoners who escaped. Wilbur, you get them looking. Most of them will be on foot. They all are wearing stripes. I want them rounded up."

"I can do that. I'm on my way."

"Good. I'm putting an all points telegram out that anyone who knows anything about the crimes will be rewarded. And telegram the Rangers in Austin for their help. Then we'll start learning who these killers were and how they came in here."

"Was it all planned, do you think, to get the brothers out of jail?" Wilbur asked.

"I really think now that it was. The robbery might have been to pay for it."

Wilbur narrowed his eyes. "But why murder his family?"

"No witnesses." It was that simple. "Don't go look inside. It's too bloody. I about puked and still may. Go get the prisoners gathered and I'll handle this."

"Should I get a tracker?"

He nodded. "Maybe two, case they've split up. But we can decide about a posse later."

Wilbur winced. "I'm sorry. But Dell, what kind of men kill kids and their mother?"

"The most absolute worst devils ever walked on this earth did this and I intend for them to pay for it."

"Hey, you want me to get you a horse?" Wilbur asked.

He shook his head. He needed some time to clear his mind. "I'll meet you at the jail."

Wilbur went for his own horse and swung aboard. "I can handle the prisoner recovery."

Dell waved him on and started up Main Street, followed by all of the curious onlookers. A block away from the bank, Guinn walked up coming from the side street and spoke to him.

"Sheriff Hoffman, how's his family?"

He shook his head and removed his hat, coming to a halt. "I'm sorry, Guinn. His family has all been murdered. Julie and the children, all of them. I just came from their house."

"Oh, my dear Lord."

He caught her. She stiffened her knees and he held her by the shoulders until she could stand.

"Why?" she said with a sob.

"No idea. They also broke all the prisoners out of the jail." He nodded to her sister

19

Nan, standing with her under the stars.

"The Cody brothers got away?" Guinn asked.

"All of them, I guess, except those too drunk to run away."

"I'm sorry to be so upset, but why would they kill them?"

"I don't know, Guinn. It is too hideous to even discuss."

"Thanks."

He squeezed her tightly once, then left her and her sister, Nan Stafford, there in the street. He hated to be so abrupt with the two women, but his mind was in a whirlwind wide as a Texas dust devil. Thomas City was the quiet seat for Saddler County in west Texas, a place where God-fearing folk lived, the local businesses serving the town folks' families and the ranches spread through the country. Outside of the Cody brothers, who'd been tried and found guilty of murdering a man they didn't like, crime was all but nonexistent. Misdemeanors, land disputes, and drunken scuffles. Nothing like this.

He couldn't believe a pack of strangers had slipped into town, taken Arnold Thompson prisoner, used his family as leverage to make him open the big green safe in his small bank — then shot him down and fled. Gunshots distracted his jailer, who rushed to back the marshal while the rest of the gang had simply walked in and gave everyone a pardon. No doubt they had horses waiting for the brothers to ride out of town, too. In the confusion of so many fleeing felons and drunks, they'd had plenty of time to escape.

Son of a bitch. This was going to be one damn big mess for him to ever straighten out.

Two

Thirty minutes later, Dell met with Billy Lee Horne, the justice of the peace, at the bank. Doc Kelton, the town's physician/medical examiner, was there, too.

Doc removed his glasses and cleaned them with his shirttail. "Billy Lee, we still have to go up to the house."

"Wait, I've seen it. It's so bloody and obscene, we may all need a drink or two of whisky to face that —" Dell dropped his head. "His death was bad enough, but his family is an even greater shame — so bad I about puked. So go warned. Nothing up there that won't shock you."

"Sheriff, can we remove his body now?"

He looked at the town's undertaker, Willis Grant's son Kent. "Yes, we have the information we need. We'll be some time up at Thompson's house. The bodies of his children and his wife are up there, Kent."

"I'll be ready for that, sir."

"Just wanted to warn you."

Billy Lee stopped Dell. "My brother's gone for a bottle. We can drink it in here and not with all those people going to troop up there along with us."

"Good idea." Dell took a seat on the edge of Thompson's desk. "Boys, someone scouted this out. They knew all about the Thompson family, the bank, even the jail. Someone filled them in ahead of time about our town, our habits, and how to get it done. This was not the work of some out-of-work cow-punchers. These are disciplined, cold-blooded killers we're dealing with, and somehow the Cody brothers are involved. I want them, and the creature who gave us all up, to hang for these murders."

"Dell, you figure he rode with them?"

He shook his head. "No, but he shares their guilt and I want him to face justice, too."

Billy Lee's brother arrived with a bottle of whiskey. Doc took the tin cup and filled it to the brim. "I can't imagine any person in this community doing that, but someone must have."

"That's the only way they could have done it."

"Do you think one of those escaped prisoners will point out the person who unlocked the cells?"

Dell pushed his hat up and nodded, taking the cup of whiskey as it was passed around the table. After a sip of the good rye, he nodded. "We'll know who that was in twenty-four hours. Where's his cashier?"

"Robert Brown? Kerrville. His mother is dying."

"I'll wire him to come back," Billy Lee said.

"Good. He'll have to straighten all this banking business out. He's the only one knows how it worked."

They downed the rest of their liquor. Giving the empty cup back to Jake, Dell led the way back outside. He stopped on the boardwalk to speak to the crowd gathered in the street.

"My friends . . . we've been visited by a terrible tragedy this night. You all know by now about the death of Mister Thompson. He was shot and killed in the bank after opening the safe at gunpoint. What you don't know, though, is that he wasn't the only one to die tonight. Whoever these animals are, they killed Thompson's whole family, too — his wife, his daughter, and both his boys."

Someone gasped, and a murmur ran through the crowd. Many of the hushed voiced asked the very same question — why?

Dell continued before they got any more skittish. "We don't know why. We don't know hardly anything yet. But it's such a horrific crime, no one will be allowed in the house until further notice. I will be back in my office, midday tomorrow. If you know anything about these outlaws, or anyone who scouted the town for them, come by and tell me what you know. In the meantime, Mister Thompson's body has been removed from the bank, Billy Lee and Doc have surveyed the scene, and they'll hold a hearing to rule on it soon."

"Will you take a posse after them, Sheriff?"

"Too early to tell. I won't take family men out in the Texas brush to get bushwhacked in the dark. These outlaws are serious killers, so ruthless you can't even imagine. I've sent for the Rangers. This is was a carefully planned, brutal crime. Go home, sleep with your guns, but don't shoot anyone by mistake. When we know more, we'll inform you. Thanks for your support and caring."

"What about the bank?" someone shouted.

"I understand his cashier, Robert Brown, is in Kerrville tonight to see about his sick mother and will be back tomorrow. He's already been sent for. The safe is empty. I know many of you had money there. We'll do all we can to help you recover it."

"Thank you, Dell," a chorus sounded off. He decided that at least part of the crowd seemed to be headed home. Satisfied, he turned and led Doc and Billy Lee up the street toward the Thompson house. Jake had already agreed to guard the bank's front door overnight to keep anyone out. Dell didn't want the bank sacked by desperate, frightened people who would ruin the books before the matter could be settled and create more confusion.

The two blocks were the longest he could ever recall walking. The day's heat had vanished, but it was hardly cold or even cool. It was a summer night of crickets chirping and some hoot owl calling. Upset dogs barked in the darkness, aroused by all the people milling about in the night.

He trudged up the front stairs with heavy steps. "All their bodies are upstairs. Just know that I warned you."

"This has damn sure been a disturbing night," Doc said. "You being a lawman, I never envied your job, but we both must pay the price for this mess."

They lit a pair of lamps near the front door and proceeded up the wide stairway to the second floor balcony looking over the living room. Shadows played eerily across the walls and would have been spooky enough in the best of times, but the silence almost hurt his ears.

Dell took one step at a time in his Kansas handmade Hyer boots. Reaching the landing, he walked through the open door and held the lamp up to light Mrs. Thompson's bloody naked corpse thrown across the stark white sheets.

"Oh, Dell. This is the worst thing I've ever saw," Billy Lee said, and quickly turned away.

Doc set about to examine her body. "You think they told Thompson if he didn't open the safe they'd kill his family?"

"I'm sure of it. And knowing the man, I'm also sure he refused them. At least at first. He was tough for a banker, but what would you do if they told you your family would die before your eyes?"

"Nothing he could do but take them down there thinking he'd cooperate and at least save them," Billy Lee said from back by the doorway.

"I bet he wasn't halfway to the bank when the ones they left behind started in on her and the children. They didn't intend to leave any witnesses."

"They didn't ride horses down to the bank?"

"No, the town marshal would've noticed. They went afoot, waited till he'd passed on his rounds, then had Thompson unlock the door. Once the safe was open, they shot him and met up with their mounts outside. Hanks was down at the livery, didn't know a thing was going on. He heard commotion and ran to the bank. Guy Branch, my jailer, locked the front door and came on the run to help him. With him gone, they just walked on in and let the prisoners out — had horses for the Cody boys and everything. They probably all went in different directions. Thirty prisoners running all over would be enough to discourage chasing them."

"The key to the jail?" Billy Lee asked.

Dell shook his head. "It was a common key. Who wants in a jail? And even if the prisoners could get out of their cells, it only locked from the outside."

Doc straightened up from his exam. "They sure raped her before they killed her, no doubt about it. More than one, from the looks of things."

"Next one's worse, Doc. The kids are in the next bedroom." Dell led the way again. Doc followed, but Billy Lee held back.

"Aw shit, Doc, do you really need me for this? I can't bear to look —"

"I can handle it, Billy Lee. Go on downstairs."

"Thank you. Dell, you've handled this the best that any man could have done."

"Goes with the job, Bill, but thanks."

"God bless you."

"When you go down, tell Kent Doc's examined Missus Thompson's body and he can remove it."

"Yes, sir." Billy Lee nodded and retreated down the stairs.

Dell turned back to the task at hand, held the lamp high for Doc to examine the little broken bodies tossed around the room like ragdolls. The physician was as professional and thorough as he'd always been, but the look in his eye told Dell he'd been shaken to the core.

"Okay, Doc?"

"I can't — what kind of animal does this, Dell? My God, I delivered all these children. They harmed no one. No one!" Doc shook his head, and Dell watched a tear run down his cheek. "Lord, what a mess."

He reached out and grasped his friend by the shoulder. "It'll take time, but we'll get these bastards, Doc. All of them."

"I hope so."

"They raped the daughter, too. Judy."

"I figured so. Makes me sick."

"I've never seen such a horrific crime." Doc began gathering up his tools. "I'll write all this up and let the boy have the bodies. It'll be one big sad funeral."

"Seen all you need to see?"

"Yes. I —"

"What's that?" When Doc had moved from beside the bed, Dell spotted something on the floor, reflecting the light of the lamp.

"Huh?"

He pointed. "That."

Doc bent over, picked up a shiny piece of metal and held it up to the light. It was a silver spur rowel.

Dell let out a low whistle. "This was handmade and cost some bucks. It's pure silver."

"Who lost it?"

"Good question. Find a match to this one and we'll have ourselves the killer, I bet."

Dell pocketed the rowel and took one last look around. Time to go. Outside, he shook both men's hands and told them he'd be at the jail if they needed him.

The sun was coming up and he still had lots to do. He hoped Guinn got some sleep in her own bed. Might be hard for anyone to sleep knowing what horrors had come to pass last night in this once quiet town. His next problem to solve was the return of the prisoners who got away. He had two bank robbers being held for the Dallas sheriff to come for them. After the Cody brothers, they were the next most desperate ones. Hale and Kempt were their names. Some ex-cowboys, he figured, but they needed to be recovered. He let out a big sigh and flexed his stiff back — there would be lots of work. Guinn'd understand — she'd have to. Maybe he could find a way to make it up to her some way. He'd try.

The public had already brought in ten prisoners. Most were serving short sentences. One guy was caught wearing a dress and sunbonnet. He might have got away, but the man who caught him noticed that it was his wife's dress and ran him down, tackled him, and then brought him in to the jail.

Two horses and saddles were reported stolen from Erv Hines's place on the north edge of town. He figured the two Dallas-bound prisoners had gotten them. More things would be found missing when folks got up in the morning.

Sitting at his desk for a moment an hour later, he looked up to see Nan coming with a covered tray of food. "My lands, what next?"

"Sis and I watched you go by and knew you never stopped for any food."

"Tell your sister, and you too, thank you, we're grateful. Caine hasn't eaten either."

"No problem. It isn't much. But it may get you two to lunch. I'll get my tray later."

"No, Nan. I'll have someone to put it on your front porch," Wilbur said.

"Well, thanks. Better eat while it is still warm."

When she was gone, his man said, "Both those women are such nice people. You ever heard where Guinn's man went?"

Dell shook his head. "She never said."

Caine looked around. "Rumor is Howard Moore run off with the Kelly girl."

"I don't know." Dell dismissed it.

"Kind of a shady deal, huh?"

"If he did that. He's been gone, what, six months?"

"Longer than that now. Why in the hell would he run off with some teenage girl when he had a pretty wife like Guinn waiting at home for him?"

"Beyond me, Wilbur. Way beyond me what he did or didn't do. How are we doing on prisoners return parties?"

"I have six sets of three or four volunteers

all on horseback, and all deputized to help find them. I believe they'll round up all the easy ones."

"Most won't be armed yet. I hope they're careful. We've had enough deaths in this town."

"Dell, there's nothing you could've done."

Dell raised a finger to make a point. "There was either someone lived here or came here and planned all this out for them. It was a split-minute timed plan. They waited for Hanks to check that end of town and get clear down the two full blocks to the livery. Then they swept in the bank. Had Thompson open it, cleaned it out, and at the final moment shot him. The horse holder arrived by then and they mounted up and rode like hell. They shot Thompson last because they knew the horses were there to ride away on and they needed a commotion to draw Hanks down there. Guy knew that he was alone, so he locked the jail to run down and help him. All natural things for them to do. They shot Thompson to draw Marshal Hanks down there so they then could empty the jail to get the Cody boys out."

They started eating their breakfast of two large flour tortilla-wrapped scrambled eggs, cheese, fried sweet peppers, and onion. Two apple Danishes were on the tray for them as well.

"I have to admit they needed lots of information to make it work. A drifter here for just one or two days couldn't plan it so well," Wilbur said between bites. "Someone drew them a map."

"Sure as hell looks that way. Wilbur, we're going to have to interrogate the prisoners about who unlocked the cells. But I think both of us need to sleep a few hours and come back fresh in the morning. Who've we got to sub for you here tonight?"

"Chris Davis. He can hold it down. He'll write down who they bring back in and handle the jail food until Guy wakes up."

"Fine. If we don't get some sleep, we'll both collapse. I don't think we can do anything with both of us done in."

"I'm going to sleep at the stables here in town — in case —"

"Not a bad idea, but get some sleep. We have lots to do."

Davis was left in charge, and Dell walked to his house the back way to avoid any conversations. He came through the back-yard gate, went inside, and got a drink at the kitchen hand pump. Then he shed his holster and gun, put it on the wall peg. Upstairs he unbuttoned his shirt and then sprawled face down on the bedspread she'd made up before she left. Neat lady — he smiled thinking about her, closed his eyes, and went to sleep.

"Dell. Dell, wake up, I need to pull off your old boots. You'll sleep better and you're making the bedspread all dirty."

"Guinn, I'm fine."

"Come on, big man." She was twisting his boot. It came off and she laughed. After the next one was on the floor, she made him get up, swept the bed covers open. Standing before him she undid his belt to let his pants fall and shoved his shirt off. "Now lay down."

"You coming?"

"Go back to sleep." She was undoing her dress. "I want to guard you. You must be worn out."

"Hold me," he said, almost back to sleep.

"That's why I came."

"When will your divorce be final?"

"February."

"I may not wait that long."

"Silly," she said and scooted up to press herself to his back. "You haven't waited at all." Then she rose up, leaned over, and kissed his cheek. "Sleep."

He knew she had no clothes on and

smiled about it falling asleep. That was how tired he was.

THREE

Nice to have Guinn there when he awoke. He went over the details of the crime with her lying at his side, squeezing his hand. "The link I need is who planned the whole thing — someone local may have done it. I can't recall any strangers hanging around and mapping all those things like the marshal's usual pattern. I bet he does it like that every night. He's a good man, but we tend to do things like we did them yesterday, don't we?"

"You mean like me and this bed?"

He half rose up and frowned at her. "That's different."

"I know it is. Go on. I'm listening to how a lawman thinks."

"What do you think about this crime?"

Guinn shrugged. "I'd never dream that a bunch of shabby outlaws would commit such a step-by-step caper."

"The entire thing was set up like a watch

works and they knew exactly how every one of us would react. Me included."

"Do you think that the Cody brothers' escape was the original plan?" she asked.

"At first, I thought they were just plain bank robbers. Now, though. . . ."

"You think a family member is involved?"

"They may be. There ain't a one of them smart enough to have planned this by themselves, though."

Guinn rolled over and rose up on her elbows. "I really appreciate you confiding in me and talking about things like you do. I could never have figured all this out, but you're right, that Cody bunch are stupid hillbillies."

"Tell me the truth. You're seeing the worst incident I've ever handled in law enforcement work. Do you still want to be the sheriff's wife?"

"This case is bad, but I know you'll solve it. It doesn't shake my belief in you as a man to be around and share my life with. This has been — I mean our affair — has been the very delight of my entire life. You listen and talk to me. Those are things Howard seldom did." She pushed her hair back from her face. "So yes, I sure want to be your wife."

Dell turned on his side and wrapped her

38

in a hug. "Great. I'm happy to hear it. I need a bath and a shave."

"I think there's something else you need to take care of here first, Sheriff."

He laughed in agreement and pulled her even closer.

Two hours later, Dell returned to the jail, where he and Wilbur sat down to interrogate the latest returned prisoner. They handcuffed Ruff Carey to a wooden chair and shot questions at him. The whiskered, bulldog-faced man was serving time for minor burglary, and he clammed up quick when they demanded to know who'd opened all the cells the night before.

"What was his name?"

"I didn't know him. It was dark. He never lit no lamps."

"What did he wear?"

"Clothes."

Dell rolled his eyes. "Well at least he won't catch a cold. What kind of clothes, jackass?"

"Regular clothes."

"What else did you see or hear?"

"He had spurs, I know that. I heard 'em jingle."

Dell and Wilbur shared a look. "Anything else?"

"I do recall hearing Otis say, 'About time you got here.' "

39

"Otis as in Otis Cody?"

"That's the one."

"Did Otis call him by name?"

"No."

"But you say the Cody boys expected him?"

"Sounded that way. That's what you thought, wasn't it? That those fellers came especially for them?" Carey laughed, showing a mouthful of rotten teeth. "Them two Dallas bank robbers asked for horses, too, but the guy who did the jail locks said, 'You two better go steal some. We don't have any extras.' I guess he warn't there for them, huh?"

"You may be right. How tall was the man turned you out?"

"Five foot eight. He wasn't big. No whiskers. He was a white guy, though. Not Spanish."

"And no names mentioned?"

"Dell, I was cutting a trail to get the hell out of here, you know? I didn't hear no more."

Dell sighed. "Put him back, Wilbur. The judge'll give him six months more for escaping jail."

"Aw, shit, Dell." Carey's shoulders dropped. "I told you everything I knowed."

"Carey, that's the law. Did you see any-

40

thing going on with the brothers that they knew about this coming off?"

"I thought them two expected a reprieve soon. Started about three weeks ago, when that Rawlins whore come by to visit."

"Tilly Rawlins?"

"Yeah."

Dell looked hard at his prisoner. "How did they act different?"

"First I thought she was going to treat 'em with her body the night before they's hung." Carey cackled like an old crone. "Now I think she told 'em someone was gonna bust 'em out."

"That cut your added term to only three months more. What else?"

Carey turned his handcuffed hands open and whispered. "I'll get you more information. I got ways. Will that cut that sentence more?"

"I'll do all I can." Dell waved to Wilbur, who stood, uncuffed the man, and escorted him back to his cell.

"You believe all that?" Wilbur asked when he got back to the office.

"I don't know what to believe yet. I damn sure want more information on this whore, though. She may be their contact."

"Damn, it sure gets deeper fast doesn't

41

it?" The deputy shook his head hard, like to clear it.

"If Carey saw that happening — and he ain't the brightest person in the jail — who else saw the change? And why didn't we?" From the open window came the sounds of riders pulling up outside. "I think they've brought some more prisoners."

"I can handle that, Dell. Take a break. We've been talking to these dumbbells all day." Wilbur moved toward the door, but stopped short. He turned back, his face thoughtful. "I think Carey told us the truth, though. I never noticed any change, but he damn sure saw it."

"So they had a month to plan things while the brothers waited out the legal challenges to their sentences."

"But they knew about it coming on three weeks ago, if Carey's right."

"Looks that way. Tilly Rawlins, huh?" Dell rubbed his tired face with his fingers. "She's up at Pettigrew's camp, isn't she?"

"Last I knew, she was treating men in a tent up there."

"Was Otis Cody having an affair with her, do you think?"

"I wouldn't bet against it. She's a whore, but I think she was soft on him. We going to start with her?"

"May as well. I doubt we learn much, but we can ride up there and check her out." Dell had little hope in any help from that visit, though. That girl would be a real hellcat to mess with. She'd sure cuss him out if he questioned her.

"All we know is that one man released them in the dark, and he was a stranger to all of them but the Cody boys."

Dell nodded. "I bet Otis didn't know him. He just knew he expected rescuers and they were late coming."

"That could be it too."

"Time may tell us. When Guy Howard gets here, you go home and get some rest. I'd hoped to learn more than we have so far. No one reported them passing through their territory, so they scattered and left the area. But they'll need to get together sometime to split that bank money, and we need to be there."

"Off the top of your head, where would they go?"

"If it was me and I was under a Texas death sentence? I'd head for Mexico."

Wilbur nodded. "Probably be the smartest thing to do."

Dell waved him away and tramped four doors down to the Longhorn Saloon. Parting the batwing doors, he let his eyes adjust to the shadowy room. Ertle McCarty was behind the bar polishing glasses.

"Evening, Sheriff. Busy day?"

"Too damned busy. You still selling cold beer?"

"I am, sir. Folks been talking how that cashier Harry Brown didn't come back today." He pulled the handle down on the tap and filled a beer mug.

"Can't do much until he returns. And he doesn't have a racehorse to ride. No more cowboy than he is, it'll take him two or three days getting back here."

Ertle nodded.

They were alone in the saloon while Dell sipped his beer. "You see anyone measuring things here in town in the past couple weeks? Any strangers?"

"Nobody I even suspected. You think they had a spy here to case the town?"

"They did do too much based on our regular habits. You closed early Wednesday night, didn't you? Slow night for business?"

"About seven that night I turned the lights out. No customers. Walked up to my house and never saw anyone. They must have popped up like mushrooms."

"Think about a spy we didn't notice."

"I'll do that, Dell. Have a good night."

Tired and aching, Dell climbed the steps

to his house and wondered if Guinn was still there. Tonight of all nights, she was just what he needed. Thankfully, it wasn't long before he saw her smiling in the kitchen door, wearing an apron, rushing to greet him with a kiss.

"You learn much today?" Her hands around his neck, he studied her handsome, sculpted face.

He filled her in on everything Ruff Carey had said, including the way Otis Cody had greeted the strange man in the jail. "That alone confirms my theory the bank robbery was to pay for their release. And the fact that the one who opened the cells told the Dallas bank robbers he had no horses for them. He wasn't there for them."

"Who was the woman told Cody the news?"

"Tilly Rawlins. She's a whore, lives down Homer Pettigrew's way. But hear tell she's been sweet on Otis for a long time."

Guinn hugged him again, then took his hand. "Supper is about ready. Let's sit down in the living room for a few minutes and tell me what happens next."

Seated on the sofa with their hands clasped, he tried to figure how to start to tell her his plans. "I'm going to face her tomorrow. That woman won't do anything

45

to help me, but I need some answers. Perhaps by her answers, I can learn if she was the one pointed out everything for them."

"That will be tough." With a soft chuckle, Guinn shook her head. "Just don't let her seduce you, though. She must be good at that."

"Guinn, I won't be tempted."

"I know. But fighting outlaws is different than getting the truth from a lying temptress. I don't doubt your devotion to me. She could shoot you in the back, you know that?"

"Yes, I know. And I'll go there with caution."

"Let's eat. Maybe let our hair down tonight, huh? Try to forget about all the bloodshed here?"

Dell grinned. "I'm so glad to be home and to have you here to greet me. Let's do that."

After supper they stood kissing in the dark kitchen. After a while, he pulled away. "Set the alarm clock for four a.m. That's an old Ranger trick. We used to go arrest outlaws before the sun came up. They're sleepy and less resistant to being arrested."

"We can do that. Just don't get shot."

"I won't."

"Put out the lights down here. I'll wind

the alarm and get up to make you break-fast."

"Thanks. Someday we won't have to sneak around. We'll be husband and wife. I promise you."

Lights out, they went upstairs to bed. He tried not to think about the wildcat he'd tangle with at dawn. Thank God he had Guinn's intoxicating body that hot night. He needed to forget what problems might await him with that lady devil out at the camp.

FOUR

Mourning doves cooed in the first cool light of dawn. Dell sat astride Burt, his Steel Dust horse, back in the cedars, listening to the campground come to life. He knew the Rawlins woman in question lived in a wall tent marked *Tilly's Love House,* but he didn't yet know which one. As the sun began to make the eastern sky rosy, though, it gave enough light to read the letters on the sun-browned canvas tent ahead of him.

He hitched Burt in the sappy boughs of the cedar tree, alongside the second horse he'd brought to take Rawlins in on if it became necessary. Jerking his rifle from its scabbard, he kept the gun against his leg so as to be out of sight should someone look up, and set out for the tent. He hadn't seen anyone up and around so far, but you could never be too careful.

When he got to the tent, he found the flaps tied shut on the inside. Shifting the

Winchester to his other hand, he drew his blade and cut through them in one quick motion. He replaced the knife in its sheath, then ripped the flaps back with the rifle barrel, finding two naked, startled people on the pallet.

"Don't you scream, now. I'll silence you with my gun."

A skinny white man, gray hair sticking out like a rooster's feathers, jumped up from the cot and charged toward him. "Get outta here, you son of a bitch! Or I'll —"

Dell clubbed him across the face with the rifle butt, and the wiry little bantam dropped like a sack of flour.

"Who do — do you want?" Tilly Rawlins cringed down behind the cot, looking up at him with wide eyes.

"You. Get dressed. You're under arrest for murder."

"Me? *Murder?*" She shook her head, like a wild animal trapped in a hole. "You can't arrest me for murder. I never killed anyone. I'm a whore. I please men, not kill them."

"Get dressed," he repeated in a low voice. "You've been implicated in the murder of Arnold Thompson and his entire family."

"I don't know nothing about that murder."

"I'm not the judge, so it's not for me to

decide. You'll have a trial, but I have eyewitnesses said you told Otis Cody they were coming to bust him out. That involves you as an accessory. If found guilty, you'll hang."

Swearing lustily, she scurried to the back of the tent and started pulling on clothes. Dell rolled her stunned partner over on his belly, then handcuffed him and gagged him with his kerchief to shut his foul mouth up.

"How will he get loose?" she asked.

"He can come to town and I'll unlock him. Then he can tell me all he knows about you and the killers."

"How's he going to ride a horse like that?"

"Come in a wagon. I don't care. It's you I'm worried about. Better take along anything you need. I've got a horse for you to ride, and you can set out your time in jail until you remember what it was you told Cody three weeks ago that made him such a happy man. Like that he and his brother was about to get sprung."

"I swear to God I never done that."

"I believe you swear at God a lot. Now get packed and get moving."

"I could please you right here and now," she pleaded. "And promise to come testify that I never done it when you need me."

"I'm not cutting any deals. Five people were murdered two days ago. You were involved. Get to moving."

"Hale, I'm sorry," she said to the moaning man on the ground. "He'll unlock them handcuffs at the jail."

Dell took the large, open-top cloth bag she'd packed and checked to be sure she didn't have a gun or knife hidden in it. Satisfied, he gave it back to her. "You try anything, I'll catch you, and you'll come in belly down over that horse I brought."

"I keep telling you I didn't do nothing."

"And I've got witnesses says you did."

"They're a bunch of damn liars."

He loaded her on the spare horse and they started off, pleased with how things had turned out. Nobody in the camp had come to her aid.

Headed into town, she brushed her messed-up hair, pleading at him from sweet to sour the entire trip. He ignored her. When they got to the jail, he put her in one of the two private cells just off his office, and told the new day man, Andy Lederman, to get her some breakfast.

"You can't keep me in here forever," Tilly cried. She was down to crying. Dell dismissed her. She held no appeal to him whatsoever. With no chance to clean up, she looked haggard. But then, most of her kind looked that way even when they weren't arrested and spending time in jail. He'd question her in the morning. A day and night in jail might shake her up a bit.

Andy told him ten more prisoners had been brought back so far, and no one had seen the bank cashier yet. Dell wasn't worried about that quite yet. The man wasn't riding a racehorse, nor was he any kind of horseman. But if it had been Dell, and he had to face the bank mess all by himself, he might not come back at all. There were going to be lots of mad people to deal with soon.

Best he could figure, the outlaw gang had all gone different ways once out of town, planning to meet up later for a split. He'd damn sure like to be there and stop it. But right now it was doubtful he'd ever do more than hear about it. He needed more information, and doubted she'd be any help. Still, he had to try. And that meant interrogate the whore.

Wilbur brought in five more escaped prisoners. He got word they'd been hanging around up on Teller Creek, stealing chickens from nearby farms. Dell helped his deputy return them to their cells. They were a haggard bunch, too.

"Hey, Sheriff, can I talk to you?" Wilbur asked as he locked the last one up. "In private?"

"Sure, Wilbur. Let's go back to my office."

"How 'bout out back, instead?"

What was so all-fired secret they couldn't talk in his office? He frowned.

Wilbur saw the look and raised his hands, palms out. "You'll want to hear this."

Dell shrugged. Wilbur would have his reasons. Turning, he walked out the front door and around the corner to the alleyway.

"Heard something while I was out rounding up this bunch. They say the Cody family drew all their money out of the bank over two weeks ago."

"Shame that cashier isn't back. I may go up there and look through the bank records. That shouldn't be hard to find."

"Can I go with you? I read good enough to help find them."

"Sure. Get the key to the door to the bank. It's in the drawer of my desk with a red tag on it."

Wilbur came back out with the key. "I've got it. Let's go look."

They started down the street, speaking to some passersby going back and forth about their business. Once at the bank, Dell unlocked the front door, let Wilbur in, and relocked it. They soon had the bank books on the desk in the banker's office.

"Where should we start?"

"This is the third week in May. Go to May first."

Caine flipped through to May first. His finger went down the column on the left. Dell took the one on the right.

"Charles Cody withdrew all his funds from the bank on the second of May." Dell reached for pencil and pad. He wrote down the amount $705 and the man's name. "That closed his account. He's an uncle to them."

"Rachel Combs withdrew her funds on the first," Wilbur said. "Five hundred and eight dollars and some cents. She's their aunt."

Dell marked her down. They turned the sheet and started down the next page.

"Ira Cody closed his account of four thousand dollars on the third," Dell said. "That's their grandfather."

"Where did he get that much money?"

"Damn, who told you about this withdrawal business?"

"Rip Collins mentioned it. Said we needed to look into it."

Dell agreed. "And we have. They knew the bank was going to be robbed. Now we have the evidence to prove it."

"I'd consider these good leads, right?"

"If I'd heard about these withdrawals when they made them, I'd have been on my guard. If Thompson had confided in me, he might be alive today. Them closing their accounts was a dead ringer the bank was about to get robbed. Let's look at the lock-box activity and see what that tells us."

"Think they'd really be concerned about them?" Wilbur asked.

"There's a chance, isn't there?"

"Rachel Combs closed her rent box the same day she withdrew the money."

"Maybe we need to start with her?"

"Like you did the lady of the night?"

"You bet. You better join me in the morning for this arrest. We'll need to leave about three a.m. to hit their place near dawn. Buster Combs may throw a fit, but I think she might be the one to tell us what really happened. Then we can quiz the rest of 'em."

"I'll be here on a fresh horse."

"Good. Go home. I'll check on the jail and head home myself."

"See you at the livery."

Wilbur went for his horse and Dell walked back to be sure all was in order at the jail. He checked with Andy, then knocked on the door outside Tilly's cell.

"They feed you?"

"Yeah, some slop. Get in here." She made a "come to me" sign with her fingers through the bars.

When he was close, she asked, "What in the hell do you want from me?"

"For you to tell me who told you to tell Cody they'd struck a deal to get him out of jail."

"I didn't do that."

"I have witnesses said you did. When those outlaws broke him out, Cody told the man who got him out that it was about time they finally got there. The witnesses said three weeks ago you told Otis what to expect on your visit and it changed those boys' whole attitude about being in jail, waiting for their sentence to be carried out."

"Why would I do that?"

"Someone paid you to tell him to be ready."

"Are you crazy? I had no information about that deal."

"A witness will testify you did, unless you confess and tell me all the details and who was behind it. Five people were murdered. If a jury doesn't hang you, you'll spend the rest of your life in prison as an accessory."

"You can't do that to me."

"I can, and I will. So make up your mind. I'll be back tomorrow and ask for your answer. Then I'll proceed with charges against you. Murder charges. I can tell you now, a prosecutor won't have any trouble convincing a jury you had a hand in those murders. By not reporting it, you were an accessory to the crime."

"You bastard."

"Names won't hurt me, but staying in prison for the rest of your life sure will be a dead end for you."

"You're lying to me!"

"Fine, don't tell me. But you'd better get used to bars and piss-stinking jail cells."

"Go to hell," she screamed as he left her.

Dell left orders for the jailer not to put any sick prisoners in the other private cell like they usually did. Andy agreed to tell his relief the same thing, and Dell left the jail to go home. There'd been no sign of the bank cashier so far that day. With a shake of his head at how slow things were going, he climbed his house stairs and went inside.

Guinn was reading a newspaper on the couch. She jumped up to greet him. "You're home early."

"I left early." He chuckled, squeezing her tight.

"Yes, you did. Did she turn your head?"

"No, I woke her and some old boy up

naked in bed. She isn't that great even naked."

"I'd hoped she wouldn't turn your head."

"Maybe away. Of course, she denies everything."

"Anything else?"

"Wilbur heard the Cody family took their money out of the bank weeks before the robbery. He and I found three withdrawals by family members early in May, and one aunt named Combs even quit renting her lockbox the same day. That ain't no coincidence."

"So?"

"We're going to arrest Rachel Combs in the morning as an accessory to the crimes. I think she'll talk. In the meantime, I left Miss Tilly thinking on how she might hang or spend her life in prison."

"I hope you get them all to talk."

"Me, too." He shook his head. "And the bank clerk hasn't shown up yet, either."

"Oh, boy. You *did* have bad day. Can we go upstairs? There's a good breeze this afternoon."

"Sure. Why not?" Arm around her waist, he squeezed her to his side.

"I can't believe you." She smiled, pushing her hair back from her face.

"How is that?"

"I was married to Howard Moore for seven years, and in all that time he never once came home midday to make love to me."

"That was his problem. I love your willingness to accept me when I do."

"Oh, I'd have been shocked. He brought no romance to our marriage. I'm glad he left, and if a teenage girl puts up with him, good for her."

"I need to get up at two a.m."

"Oh, yes, Ranger Dell."

"Wilbur's going along."

"Thank God. You've got a good idea there."

He stopped. "I've always enjoyed being sheriff. But the last few days, I've thought about finding a new occupation."

She stopped and frowned back at him from halfway up the stairs. "You wouldn't be happy running a store, stable, or being a teamster. Hold on. I know you'll solve this thing."

She kissed him, then led the way upstairs in a big hurry. Laughing, they undressed and jumped into bed.

At the livery early the next morning, the man who worked the stables at night had his horse and the spare saddled and ready to go.

"Dell, what're you going after tonight?"

"Another suspected criminal."

"That guy you handcuffed at Tilly Rawlins's tent got a ride in on a buckboard last night. Had a black eye he said you give him. They unlocked him up at the jail, but he said they wouldn't let him talk to Tilly. Boy, he was angry. Came out of the jail cussing you to high heaven."

"Why, that just breaks my heart."

They laughed. Out the stable door, they heard a horse coming, and Wilbur rode up on his mount. As Dell mounted up, he told the swamper to tell the bantam with the bruised ego he said to find a new girl. Tilly was going to hang or go to prison for life.

Dell and Wilbur rode off, headed northwest for the Combs Ranch on the wagon road. They passed through some cedars and live oak groves under the stars and a low half moon. They spooked some night-grazing deer along the way before crossing lots of great open grassland. Just before dawn, the shapes of the Combs house, corrals, and barns appeared out of the mist.

"They have dogs?" Wilbur asked.

"Stock dogs, I think. I was here three times trying to round up the Cody Brothers. They were never here, but I always thought Rachel hid them when I came by."

Those dogs raised a ruckus as they rode up. Pulling his Winchester, Dell reined up to one side of the yard where nobody could shoot at him without exposing themselves.

"Sheriff out here," he called. "You're under arrest. I have a posse. Both of you get out here. And don't try anything, or we'll shoot you down."

"What the hell does he want?" a man's voice demanded.

"How should I know?" a woman's voice answered.

"Get out here with your hands up," Dell yelled again, "or we'll start shooting."

"We're coming, dammit. Hold your pants on."

Old Buster Combs came out on the porch with his hands held high. Wilbur checked him for weapons, then made him lie face down in the dirt.

"Hell, she ain't going to shoot you," Combs grumbled.

Rachel Combs appeared, looking groggy, and buttoning up her dress. "I don't know why you're here."

Dell dismounted and tramped up the steps, rifle in hand. "Rachel Combs, I'm arresting you for your involvement in the recent murders, bank robbery, and jailbreak."

"What are you talking about?" Her husband started to push up off the ground, but Wilbur jammed him down with his boot in the middle of his back.

"Buster, you stay there. You want to be an accessory, I'll arrest you, too."

"How can you say she did anything like that?"

"Because I have proof she knew about the robbery before it happened. That makes her an accessory to the jailbreak and the murders of the Thompson family."

"You're crazy, Hoffman."

"Five innocent people were murdered in the bloodiest crime I know of in Texas history. A jury of her peers won't hesitate to find her guilty when they hear how terrible those murders were."

She looked terrified. "I didn't know anything about it."

"Come along. We have a horse for you to ride. I won't handcuff you, but if you try to escape, we'll haul you in belly-down and handcuffed." Dell took her by the arm, passed her off to Wilbur. The deputy guided her off the porch and headed for the horses.

"Hoffman, you won't get away with this," Buster growled. "I swear, I'll track you down and kill you."

"Combs, if you try that, you better be sure

to wear your best suit. The undertaker'll need it to bury you in."

Buster beat on the porch floor with his fists. "There's things you can't do to an innocent woman."

Dell kneeled beside the man. "On May second, she withdrew all her money from the bank and closed her lock box so it wasn't there for the robbers to steal. She knew they were coming, and so did the others in her family, because they all did the same thing. Then a paid agent went to the jail and told Otis help was on the way, for him not to worry, they'd have him and his brother out before they hanged. I intend to prosecute Rachel to the fullest extent of the law for her involvement. Of course, if those brothers come clean and surrender, we might overlook some things."

"You son of bitch. I'm gonna get a big lawyer in San Antonio who'll run circles around your prosecutor."

"When witnesses testify how those men raped the banker's wife and daughter, then cut their throats along with those of two young boys, do you really think those jurors are going to let her off when they see the bank records? It's right there in the ledger that Rachel drew out her money on purpose before it happened. She knew those outlaws were coming and who they were. She better put herself on the mercy of the law and tell us all she knows about the plans and who was involved in. You may give your ranch to that slick lawyer, but you'll lose it and her if you do."

"You —"

"I'm going to arrest all those who removed their money to save it. I don't get those boys back, along with all of those involved in this crime, then your wife's headed to prison for a real long time."

"She had nothing to do —"

"No, Buster. I have the proof. She either owns up to it, or she's done. And we'll get those killers back in the end, too."

Rachel Combs cried all the way into town. The two lawmen were not taken in by her sorrow, and had her booked in the jail by ten o'clock that morning.

Before he put Combs in her cell, he drew Tilly Rawlins out and sat her down in a chair to wait for them to interrogate her. She frowned as Wilbur took the other crying prisoner into the other private cell.

"What's the matter with her?"

"She's going to prison with you. She knew all about the robbery and murder ahead of time, too. If she agrees to testify against you, though, she may save herself years in jail or hanging."

"She don't know one gawdamn thing about me."

Dell shook his head. "She knows all about it. I have the proof on her, and she'll make a witness against you to save herself. When she does, it'll be too late for you to admit you knew all about the deal and your trial will proceed. She's their aunt."

"I know who she is. That bitch is going to testify against me?"

"You're starting to get it right."

"Aw, hell, I never done nothing."

"What can she lose? I have her dead to rights over the money she took out of the bank. She knew they were coming to rob it and break her nephews out."

Tilly wilted, dropped her shoulders. "I'll tell you about the deal. I'll tell you everything I know. Will that get me off?"

Dell shrugged. "Might. Sit there. I'm getting Wilbur. I want to put all this down on paper and have you sign it before I agree to anything. I warn you it better be the truth."

She made a sour-looking face and lowered her voice. "Listen, I said I'd tell you all I know. Lots I don't know, but you can have all that I do."

Wilbur came in the front jail door and Dell told him to go get Billy Lee. His deputy smiled and left on the run. Twenty minutes later, with Dell doing the writing and Wilbur and Billie Lee there as witnesses, Tilly told her side of the story.

"I've always been kinda sweet on Otis. Christopher, his younger brother, is a no good bastard, but that was my opinion. After they shot that guy, they were on the run — you know that. Hell, you're the one ran them down, at the old Lister place. I'd met up with Otis there the night before. The dumb son of a bitch should have lit out for Mexico. I told him you'd be there soon, but he brushed it off."

"You met him there?"

"Yes. I left just before sunup. Probably passed you creeping up on the place."

"You were helping them hide out?"

"No. I just slept with him. The family must have sent them food and supplies." She sniffed. "After that, I had to find me a new place to entertain men. So I went to Pettigrew's Camp."

"That was the last time then?" Dell asked.

"Yeah. You had their trial and the jury come back and said hang them."

"There's more to tell us about your involvement."

"Yes. I didn't hear any more until his

grandfather came and paid me to go see Otis."

"He paid you?'

"Yeah, but that white hair on his head ain't snow on a mountain. You know what I mean?"

"I think I do. He paid for your services?"

"Two bucks for me, and five more to go tell Otis they — he meant the family — had a plan to get them out. He told me to say none of the family could go to jail to visit. Ira said that would make you suspicious, and he was right."

"Damn right," Dell agreed. "I wondered why they didn't come see them. But lots of activity would have aroused my suspicions even more."

"First few trips, I just went. Told Otis the reason why the family didn't come. Then Ira came over to my tent for an all night stay. You don't need that part wrote down. He got to drinking moonshine while we were in bed, and he said they found the men they needed — but the family didn't have enough money to pay them for the job. They wanted ten thousand dollars to do it. Ira kept cussing how he didn't have that much money.

"I told him Otis was really down about nothing being done to spring them. Ira was on top of me that night doing his thing and in my ear said, 'They'll never hang, Tilly. If I have to rob every blessed bank in Texas. My boys' — he called them that — 'they ain't going to hang. I have help coming. When you go to see him, tell him that secret-like so no one knows they're coming.'

"That's all I know. You know I'm a whore and we aren't worth much. Any one of the Codys would've cut my throat if I'd told you a thing. Hell, they still may do that. I never heard who the men were, or when they'd come. That's all I know, so help me God. I never dreamed they'd murder that family or even rob the bank. All I expected was for the gang to show up and break Otis and Christopher out of jail. That's it."

There came a knock at the door. Wilbur got up and checked who it was.

"Dell, two Texas Rangers are here."

Dell nodded at the two men who came in, then checked the clock. In an hour the mass funeral would start. They'd kept the bodies in the icehouse so some relatives could make the services. He regretted all morning how Guinn would have to attend it with Nan and her husband, Ralph Stafford.

"Is that all you know?" Dell asked her.

"Yes, sir."

"Tilly, I have to go to the funeral. No time

to change my clothes, but I'm going to have Bess Clark buy you a real dress and take you over to the hotel to get you a bath. Then I'll have someone take you back to your camp in the morning. Fair enough? Don't leave the county, or tell that woman in the other cell a thing about this confession. If you do, I'll tear it up. Now sign it."

"I've had a boy go get Burt for you to ride out to the funeral," Wilbur said. "You better get out there now."

The two Rangers introduced themselves as Alan Smith and Hiram Lake. Dell explained quickly about Tilly's confession, then how Wilbur would show them the crime scenes while he went to the funeral. He would meet them afterward at their rooms at the Gladstone Hotel down the street.

With that, Dell went out, mounted Burt and headed off toward the rise east of town. There was lots of traffic in the street, and buggies, wagons, and buckboards parked all over the grassy hillside. A Methodist preacher named Ogden was to perform the services, but nothing had started yet. He dismounted and left Burt on the picket line for horses.

He saw some of Thompson's family on the front row. Removing his hat, he nodded to Guinn, her sister Nan, and Ralph, who were standing in the back. Ralph brought the women over to join him. Nan asked Dell how things were going.

"Two Rangers arrived today. Tilly made a confession before I left down there about her part in the deal. The old man paid her to tell them Otis was coming to get them out."

"Did Missus Combs talk?" Guinn asked in a whisper.

"She cried all the way here."

"I bet that was neat."

"A shame," Dell agreed. "But I think I convinced her husband if them boys didn't give themselves up, there'd be lots of that family in jail."

"The preacher's about to start. We can talk more later. You know I'm proud to stand up here with you?"

"I'd do lots more if you had the papers freeing you from him."

"I saw your wife's grave today. This must be a hard place for you to come to."

"Connie's been gone three years. At first it was hard, then I came up here alone and spoke to the wind. She was a great woman, but I fully understand she can't come back. My life is with you now."

70

"Amen. You know I'd squeeze your hand —"

"Our dear heavenly father we are here today to comfort the loved ones and friends of the Thompson family as we deliver unto God all five members of that household. . . ."

The service went on. The hot afternoon wind increased. Crows cawed louder, and somewhere a forlorn cow bawled for her calf. Horses on the picket line fought a little and a baby in the crowd cried. At last the minister completed the liturgy, and people went by to pay their respects to the family.

Dell reset his hat upon his head. "See you later."

Guinn nodded.

He hurried back to town and the jail. He paid a boy a dime to take Burt back to the stables. Dell, Wilbur, and the Rangers all went down to the saloon for a beer and to talk about things. Ertle brought them a round of beers and left them to talk.

Alan Smith started their conversation. "Sheriff, Wilbur told us how quickly you saw this crime was tied to the jailbreak. And the confession this woman gave you today ties the family in on it?"

"I knew this wasn't a case of some unemployed cowboys robbed a bank as they passed through. It was too well-planned. The murder of the family was to keep there from being any witnesses. Shooting Thompson drew the small night law force two blocks away from the jail. The confusion covered the jailbreak, and turning all the prisoners loose prevented us from trailing them. They planned it down to the minute."

Smith nodded in agreement. "We have an all points out on the Cody Brothers. Nothing so far, but if they stay in Texas, we'll capture them. And that other pair you had housed from the Dallas bank robbery."

"According to one of my prisoners, the jailbreaker told them they were on their own and he had no horses for them to ride."

Hiram Lake stirred. "That woman who confessed this morning, how much money did she say they wanted to make this jailbreak happen?"

"Sounded to me like they wanted a small fortune to pull the job off. Ten thousand dollars. So the Cody bunch must have convinced them there was lots of money in the bank safe. We're still waiting for the cashier to tell us just how much. He went to Kerrville to see about his sick mother and we sent word to him about what happened and to come back. But he isn't a cowboy, so it's taking time for him to ride back up here."

"Besides those four men, are any of the other escapees particularly dangerous?"

Dell shook his head. "Wilbur, you think any left on the list as non-returned would be dangerous?"

"No, sir. This morning we were down to nine left to recapture. My deputies are still following leads, but I think we'll capture them in a matter of days."

"So you have no idea who or where they went with the Cody brothers?" Smith wiped the beer foam from his mustache.

"All we know is they left, and I imagine on good horses. Can you two think of any situation like this where a gang came to get someone out of jail for a fee?"

"I can't. Can you Hiram?"

"I seem to recall over in Downum County a few years ago. They shot a jailer and did this very same thing. Turned them all loose to get one guy out. I'm trying to remember how that ended. I know the escapee was in a shootout later in El Paso that cost him his life, but they never found the jailbreakers."

"We have the Cody boys' aunt in our Crossbar Hotel now, too. She pulled all her money out of the bank weeks before the robbery. I suspected she sheltered them when I was running them down for their trial, too. I told her husband if he wanted his wife back to get those boys back here, or she'd be gone for a long prison term."

"What did he say?"

"That shut him up. Told me first he was hiring the best lawyer in Texas. I told him he'd lose his ranch and all his money and still not have her out of jail."

Lake laughed. "I'd shut up, too, to that kinda talk."

"Either of you know Texas divorce law? I have a woman who's been abandoned for over a year now and can't get her marriage set aside. They told her their earliest date to consider it is next February."

"I believe Court Judge Charlie Ransom at Waco could handle that for her."

"I'll write him a letter tonight."

"Tell him who you are and Ranger Alan Smith sent you. You'll get some movement on it, I bet."

"What do you two want to do here?"

"Scout around if Wilbur doesn't mind showing us some more things."

"He's yours. I may get you two to serve a warrant or two on some of the Codys while you're here, too. That might scare them out enough for us to get more information out of them." Dell stood and thanked them. "I've got the beer. Have an interesting tour."

74

"We sure hope you solve it, Sheriff. Thanks," Smith said. They shook hands around the table. Dell paid Ertle for the beer, and then walked back to the jail.

Andy grabbed him as he came through the door. "That lady came and took Tilly for a bath and a dress."

"Good. We need to hire someone to drive her up to the camp tomorrow. Did Missus Combs eat lunch?"

"All she's done is lay on her bunk and bawl out loud."

Dell opened the door to the first private cell. "Missus Combs, stand up. That's an order."

Still sniffling, Combs managed to stand, wiping her red nose on a rag.

"If you don't eat supper tonight, in the morning me and my men will feed you a bowl of cereal. It won't be nice. Do you understand?"

"I'll eat tonight."

"You better have those men's names for me tomorrow, or you'll do lots of prison time."

"I'm telling you I don't know who did it."

Dell snorted. "Your memory will clear in here as time goes on."

"You don't listen to me," she bawled. "I

don't know about anything you're talking about."

"Your memory better recover."

He told Andy he was headed home, and that Wilbur was off riding with the Rangers. Then he left and walked home.

Would Guinn be there? More and more, she came over to see him. They had such a neat affair. Maybe he could help her out on getting a divorce from that judge in Waco. For both their sakes.

"Hey," she said, coming downstairs in a flash. "I washed the sheets and they're fresh."

"Fine with me."

"Want to go up and mess them up?"

"Give me just a minute and we will. The Rangers came in today. One of them told me there's a judge in Waco who might grant you a divorce if I write and ask him for help."

They kissed and she put her arms around his neck. "What will it take?"

"I need to write him a letter. I'll do it while it's fresh in my mind."

"Pen and ink are on the desk."

Ten minutes later, the letter was finished and in an envelope to be mailed in the morning. He met Guinn back in the parlor, where she removed his hat and his gun belt and hung them on a pair of wall-mounted pegs. She kissed him fiercely, then turned and raced up the stairs ahead of him. What a crazy fun partner he had found. Maybe they could make it permanent when the letter returned from Waco.

He hoped so.

FIVE

Dell woke early, ready to go try to solve his case. Guinn poured him his first cup of coffee and asked if his latest prisoner had said anything so far. He'd told her the night before about his deal with Tilly and her confession.

He shook his head. "I still have no clue about these outlaws and I really need them — a name, a description, *something.*"

"Don't go off someplace by yourself today without Wilbur to cover your back. Promise me?"

"I'll be careful. Quit worrying about me."

"I worry because you're so upset about this thing. But you're making progress. Just don't be foolish." She bent over, kissed him, and sat down across the table to eat breakfast. "Nan and I may go to Carterville to look for some new material for dresses. We'll just go and come back, but supper may be later tonight. Is that all right?"

"No problem. You two always have fun together."

"I didn't upset you at the funeral yesterday, did I? Asking about your wife?"

"No. We have to carry on our lives and our future. I hope my letter's answered shortly. I'll send it off today."

"So do I, *hombre*. So do I."

Dell went on to the jail, mailing his letter to the judge on the way. According to Andy, Wilbur had ridden out with the two Rangers at sunup for parts unknown. Since his female prisoner wouldn't answer him about anything, he went and got Burt out of the livery and headed for Comanche Springs, another hangout for the unemployed and misfits, along with a *puta* or two who hung out there. He had little trouble with the residents there, but they were all on the shady side. Even with the carpetbagger government recently gone, Texas was still poor and jobs came at a premium. Thus, these places were hangouts for less-than-hard workers, the lame, sick, and aged. It was also on the little-used route on the old Comanche trail from raids into south Texas back to drier lands in the west.

He arrived on the site and rode through the camp of canvas- and hide-covered huts. There were a few rough log shelters, too, and some others made of scrap boards salvaged from signs. Cooking fires made smoke, and many blank-eyed Hispanic women stared at him as he passed — some pregnant, some suckling babies, they hung their washed clothes on lines in the shade of the mesquite trees. A white-bearded man rose and walked from his spot on the ground to intersect with him and his horse coming on the long well-worn ruts.

"What brings you out here, Sheriff?"

"Five murders and a bank robbery, plus a half-dozen jail escapees still loose."

"Holy shit. That all happened to you?"

"You knew that less than twelve hours after it happened. Cut the crap, Louie."

"There ain't any loose jail inmates 'round here, Dell. But the guy you are looking for has a scar on his left cheek, maybe a branding iron got too close to him."

"How do you know I want him?"

"Sheriff, I been around tough guys, but he could bite the heads off sixteen-penny nails and spit them hard enough to kill you with 'em."

"Louis, you saying he was that tough?"

"I thought so. And quick as cat with a gun, too. He drew it at a thing or two here. Faster than lightning."

"Why was he here?"

"Wanted the back wall of your jail blown off."

"You don't say. How much would he pay?"

"Two thousand dollars."

Dell whistled. "That's some payout."

"Yeah," Louie agreed. "But look, you'd put the finger on me for doing it. Why, I'd had to leave Texas. Where in the hell could I go with you on my ass?"

"How tall?"

"Five nine or so."

"Hair color?"

"Dark brown or black."

"Age?"

"Thirty-something."

"Where can I find him?"

"I'd think El Paso."

"Why there?"

"Old man Cody went out there the day after the jury found them two guilty of murder."

"He did?"

"Yes, he got on the stage and went there. They say he had a suitcase full of money to pay them."

"How much money?"

"I heard by the grapevine they wanted over ten thousand dollars up front — and no guarantee."

"Where did the brothers go after the

breakout?"

"Across the border, huh? I would beat a trail for there if you were going to hang me." He spit some tobacco in the dust, then wiped his mouth and mustache with the web of his right hand.

Dell agreed. "Any come through here?"

"If they did, they passed by at night. I never saw them. Two of the escapees were here for short time, got a little money from one of the *putas.*"

"Who were they?"

"They robbed a bank in Dallas. You arrested them."

"She give them much?"

He fixed a mangy dog sniffing his sandals with a hard kick in the ribs. The dog slipped away, yelping. "Get away you SOB, or I'll kill you. No, she had little money."

"Where'd they go?"

"She never said."

"She around?"

"No, she may have left."

Dell accepted his words, even if he didn't like them. He gave him a gold ten-dollar piece the size of a dime. The man took a buckskin pouch on a leather strap from inside his shirt and placed the coin it.

"*Gracias.* The boy has brought your horse up here for you."

"Thanks. Right or left cheek?"

His hand went to the right side of his unshaven face. His dark eyes met Dell's. "There."

"Right side." Dell took the reins and gave the shocked-faced boy a nickel, then swung up on the big horse. *"Vaya con Dios, hombre."*

The big man nodded and said to the boy, "Give me that money he paid you."

But the young boy's sandals were on fire and he outran all but the camp dogs to keep his money. Dell laughed and then rode back for town. At last he had a description, a first name, and a scar — right cheek.

Six

The two rangers huddled with Wilbur and Dell around a table in the saloon late that afternoon.

"He's got a scar from a branding iron burn on his right cheek?" Smith asked, and then glanced at his partner before sipping his beer.

Looking across the table, Lake wiped the foam off his mustache. "Why not wire the El Paso office? They may know him."

"That's a big break in the case, boss man."

Dell agreed. "Now, finding him won't be easy, but we at least have a description. Ertle, can you come over here please?"

The bartender put down his white towel and came out from behind the bar. "Need more beer?"

"In a short while. Has a man with a bad scar on his right cheek been in here lately? About medium height?"

"Yes, now that I recall. He came by one

day, had a beer, and asked me about a certain *puta,* if I could point her out to him. Don't know his name, but that scar's something you don't forget. I sent him to Angel Cordova's crib. Maybe she knows his name. I never thought about him again. Gave me a quarter and left — never drank the beer."

Dell looked over at his deputy. "Wilbur, it's your turn go find the girl and meet us at the jail. No hurry, and don't stir up any dust. We simply want to ask Angel some questions. Thanks, Ertle. Bring us three more beers."

"That was some time ago," the bartender added. "He didn't stay here long."

"I better go wire El Paso about him," Smith said. "Make it two beers, Ertle. We're hurting your business." He left to send the wire.

"Did Rachel talk any more this morning?" Lake asked.

"No she's numb and dumber than before. She's a helluva lot tougher than most men I've pried answers out of. I had my way, I'd be sticking her head in a water trough until she told me all she knew."

He laughed. "You ever done that before?"

"Hell yes, but never on a woman."

The Ranger was about to crack up laughing. "I was with Captain Jack Holt one time years ago. These Mexicans had robbed an old woman and we caught them. He asked this big, swaggering leader where they hid the loot. Captain Jack soon had all he wanted from him and ordered him drowned. Three of us set in and we took him to a horse tank, held his head under water. About the time we had him on the brink, Jack came down there, got off his horse, took that *hombre* by his hair, and lifted him out, water gushing from his mouth and anxious to tell him where it was hid. We got damn near all of it back, too."

"But there's a big difference between drowning a bandit and a woman."

"Unfortunately," Lake agreed, sour-faced.

Dell and the Ranger finished their beer and went to the jail while Wilbur looked for Angel. His man finally delivered the high-breasted Hispanic woman in the jail under a shawl that looked too warm for the growing summer heat. She swept it around her body and refused to be seated.

"Angel do you remember the man with the scar on his face?"

"Hell no."

"Think on it again, *señorita.* You stay in this town because I allow you to. Five people were slaughtered like sheep. This man may be one of the killers, and he was here, and seen in your company."

"He told me he would kill me if I told anyone he had even been here." Obviously, she'd taken his point to heart.

"Sit down. Wilbur and I'll protect you if he ever comes back. I swear you will never be hurt."

"Hmm." She swept her skirt under her and took the middle chair. "When my throat is cut, you will bring me back to life?"

Dell and the others straddled chairs backwards. "I won't let that happen. Now, what's his name?"

"Rollo."

"Rollo what?'

"Rollo Magnus."

"Why was he here?"

She shook her head.

"He told you why he came here," Dell pushed.

"He said he was here to meet a man to do business. I am not sure what business that was."

"But you remembered him when hell broke loose here?"

"I did not know what they would do. I realized then that was why he came to talk to someone that night. He had planned to rob the bank."

"Did he meet someone at your crib?"

She closed her long, dark lashes like the question pained her and nodded.

"Who?"

"Rob."

"Rob? The bank cashier?"

She nodded again. "Rob used me often. He was a customer and slipped in and out of my crib."

"I'll be damned," Wilbur slapped his hat on his thigh. "That's why he hasn't come back."

"And he won't now." *Not unless we catch him, at least.*

Dell shook his head in disgust. Did this Rollo ask Ertle for Angel, or did he point her out for him? That could all be answered, but had Robert, the bank employee, been in on it? That tore it with the bank records, too. They would have to have the state banking people come out to Thomas City and settle things.

He rubbed his face with his calloused palms. Holy shit. He damn sure never expected Rob to be involved. "I wonder what his share was."

"I did not hear them talking," Angel said, her brown eyes serious. "You know anyone can kill a whore and not even see a trial. This *hombre* Rollo smelled of death. I know what that smell is now."

"Angel, was there anyone else he wanted to see?"

She shook her head. "He came one afternoon. Rob came to meet him there after work. I went to my girlfriend's place. They talked for two hours, maybe more. A young boy knocked on the door and told me a man wanted me back at my crib. He wanted my services. Rollo paid me generously for that and then left. I never even saw his horse. Rob came by a day or two later. He was a little drunk and told me his name by mistake."

"Did he tell you he was going to check on his sick mother?"

"Yes. I even burned a candle in my church for her."

"We were all blindsided, Angel. All of us." Dell tented his hands and shook his head, thinking. "We don't know who was in the bank during the robbery. If this guy had Rob there, he'd know any place Thompson could hide money from them."

"All the more reason to kill all witnesses, too," Lake added.

"Exactly. Angel, we mean you no harm. Thank you for coming here, and if you think of more, please tell me or Wilbur."

"I will do that. *Gracias, Señor* Hoffman." She swirled the shawl around, and head held high, left the jail.

"Well, by God, we have a name. I'm wiring El Paso to find him if he's there," Smith said.

Dell grimaced at this latest revelation. "We need an all points lookout deal on Robert. Damn, and I've defended his slow return. I can't believe this. All of it going on under my damn nose and not a word."

"Dell, you had a good day," Smith said, and the others agreed. "You have two names more than you had a day ago. I have your file on Robert. I'll fill out the wanted order."

"I may need to arrest the elder Cody and quiz him. He's tough as an oak stump, but he had a hand in this."

"He can't be that tough," Lake said.

"You don't know him like I do."

"When?" Wilbur asked. "When do we bring him in?"

"I'll decide tonight. Something for me to sleep on. Thanks, everyone. We made some good strides today, despite the things that keep seeping out to our attention."

At his house at last, Dell went up the porch stairs feeling weary and given out by the days going by so fast with no one arrested for the crime. Turning the knob and opening the door, he stopped and looked the woman he had come to love so much, in her apron and ready for him. Damn, he had one lucky shining star in his gloomy life.

After supper, she made him undress. He got belly down on their bed and she worked on his back with hot wet towel compresses and her powerful hands. It eased his tight muscles and he felt relaxed for the first time in days.

"And Robert was in on the robbery?" she asked, rubbing a little deeper.

"From today's information, I'm afraid he was right in the middle of it. Damn, I never could have imagined him in league with those killers."

"How could he let them kill those children?"

"If he was here, no one saw him. He was probably at the bank when they were murdered, best as I can figure. He may have provided the information they needed to get in the bank safely and unseen with Thompson turning the dials."

"Feel better?" she asked, leaning over close to his ear.

"Honey, I'm better than I've been all day. You work wonders, I swear."

She kissed him on his cheek. "Let's go eat supper."

"I'll be dressed in a few minutes. It going

all right for you?"

"Oh, I'm fine. I know how bad this is eating you up, but you are still making progress."

"We have so few leads, though. And the fact their leader was here and no one noticed him bothers me. The dove said he smelled of death. She never explained that. I've smelled dead bodies, but not someone walking around smelling like death."

"I bet she's smelled a lot." Guinn laughed.

"I agree."

"And the Combs woman hasn't told you anything?"

"No. She's mum."

"You have some new leads, anyway."

"Yes. Maybe the Rangers in El Paso can find this man."

"I hope so." She hesitated. "I'm sorry, but I have to ask you for some money. I want to help Nan with her grocery bill this month. I had some, but I've used all of it. Ralph's saddle repair business slowed since the bank closed."

"Sure, how much do you need?"

"Oh, ten dollars. I'll sign a note."

He kissed her. "I'll take it out in trade."

"Dell, you make me out to be a shady lady."

"Honey, I'm teasing you. I love you and

you know I'd marry you right now if you were divorced. My money is your money."

"It was hard enough asking you for the money."

"Whatever is mine is yours. Don't ever hate asking me."

"I won't ever again. I simply felt bad about needing money to help pay her for putting up with me."

"That's the thing to do. I can afford our part."

"Thank you." She hugged him again. "So what are you planning on doing tomorrow?"

"Arresting the uncle and his grandfather. They can sit in jail a while. I doubt I can get them to tell me much, but maybe they'll slip up."

"I hope so. This case is endless. Does that bother you?"

"More than I can tell you. I usually can capture the criminal and lock him up fast. This deal has so many involved, I may need a larger jail."

"So this Rollo Magnus was a big find?"

"Yes. We have a chief suspect now. The Rangers will help me arrest them."

"Thank God. Maybe you won't get shot that way."

"Honey, I don't aim to get shot."

"No, you won't shoot yourself, but that

bunch might."

"I doubt that. Rangers carry a big rep for no nonsense arrests or else."

"Good luck."

He chuckled. "I wasn't making fun of our relationship. I really will help anything you need to pay. I know you're troubled being left and not being able to do anything about it."

"I'm fine. A little touchy about things like needing some money to help them for caring for me. I won't ever give my worthless husband being gone one fret. My time spent with you is ten times better than any minute I spent with him."

"I appreciate you. And we'll eventually be man and wife. I'm doing all I can."

Dressed at last, she finally coaxed him back downstairs to have supper. His back felt so much better. He could not believe her hands had done so much for him.

"You do that for him, too?"

She made a peeved face. "Yes. I should have let him suffer."

"No. I bet he misses that. And you, too."

"He doesn't care. He has that poor girl to wait on him hand and foot. He probably has her with a baby by now or when he left. We never had any children."

"I'm not worried about that. Connie and

I lost two at birth. That may be worse than not having them."

"After all those months losing them like that would be bad."

"It was."

"Dell, I know you're loaded down with this robbery and murder. Let's be brighter than that."

"I plan to start right now." He reached over and squeezed her hand. "You are my light in a dark cave."

Early the next morning he walked down to his office and spoke to folks on his way. Three of them were deputized ranchers headed out to find more of the escaped prisoners.

"I sure appreciate you three rounding up those prisoners."

"No problem, Dell. We know you're working hard to find the killers. Wilbur told us Robert was involved?"

"I could hardly believe it, myself, but obviously he may have been and that's why he never came back. The Rangers have an all-points bulletin out to arrest him."

"That Combs woman ever tell you how she was involved?"

"I intend to have her tried if she doesn't come clean."

"We heard about two of those loose prisoners that are hiding up around the old Willis place."

"I hope you get them. Be careful."

"Any time we can help you send word, Dell."

He thanked them again and went on. Max Cooper, owner of the town mercantile, was out sweeping off his porch as Dell passed.

"This bank business is hurting us all, Dell. Lots of folks lost money, but it'll be like dominos in the months ahead."

"I know, Max. You know if I could go seize the money they stole, I would."

"I know that. I simply don't know how we we'll make it."

Dell clapped him on the shoulder. "I can do anything for you, let me know."

The man didn't try to answer. He simply nodded — lips tightly drawn in a line.

He went on, sick to his stomach. If a merchant like Cooper was that hard hit, others would be, too. Damn, this got worse and worse — and he had no solution. He'd sent Wilbur off with one of the Rangers to arrest the uncle. He'd take the other lawman and go for Ira in the morning.

Later in the day, he and Hiram Lake cross-examined Rachel Combs again. She stubbornly protested them. A tall, thin woman in her late thirties with graying hair, she'd never had any children of her own. At least not any that Dell knew about.

"You met with this man Rollo, the one who came from El Paso to plan the robbery and jailbreak."

"Who said that?"

"I have lots of witnesses."

She wilted a little at his words. Sensing the breaking of the dam, Dell pressed on. "Did he make love to you?"

Sitting up straight and acting defiant, she said, "They lied about that."

"Does your husband know about it?"

"He knows nothing — whoever told you I did that?"

He saw a new woman sitting in the chair. "I have lots of people saw things you aren't telling me. You and him have a long affair?"

"No."

"But you did have one with him?"

"He raped me."

"You tell your husband he did that?"

"No, and don't you tell him, neither."

"Why did you not tell him he did that to you?"

She began to cry. "Those brothers were like the boys I never had. I admit I'd do anything for them. I couldn't help they shot that man. They were wild boys, but I didn't want them to die. I lost several children in my marriage. If you promise not to tell anyone, I mean anyone, about my being raped — I'll tell you what I know."

Dell glanced over at Lake. He was seated on a kitchen chair backwards and nodded.

"I promise to keep that secret, but I want to know everything about this crime, you hear me? Everything."

"My husband must never know. I didn't do that business with him willingly, but Buster might not believe I couldn't help myself in that case."

"I understand."

"Those people from El Paso wanted twenty thousand dollars to get them boys out of jail and away from here. None of us had that much money, so this Rollo you talk about came here in secret. He stayed at my house three days, because my father and brother said you wouldn't check there. I was told to have Buster clear out for those days, so he'd have no part of what they were planning, and to feed Rollo while he was there."

Rachel swallowed, shook her head. "I stayed outside as much as I could. I didn't want to hear any of what they were planning. But I knew without getting them boys out, they'd hang. Each night Charles and Dad went home and left me with that cruel bastard — who raped me every night. And he laughed about it." She dropped her chin, fighting back more tears. "You know when you deal with the devil, you will have more problems. I was the brunt of that. I have never been unfaithful to my husband, but he would never understand what happened."

"How much did they pay him in total?"

"All the money I had in the bank. I gave him some gold jewelry that my aunt gave me from my strong box. My brother gave him all he had. My father paid him two thousand dollars in El Paso, and two more when he came here."

"How did Robert the cashier get involved?"

"Otis and Christopher knew him before they were arrested. Knew he was not paid anything at the bank, and might help them if he got a share of bank robbery. He knew the safe combination if Thompson refused to open it. So they cut him in to be sure the safe would be opened. No one ever mentioned killing Thompson or his family. That was their business. I only wanted my boys free. I never wanted Rollo to assault me, neither."

Dell shook his head. "You've paid a high price for all this, Rachel, but you're still guilty of a heinous crime. People around here'll probably never recover financially from the bank's failure to pay them. Those two boys were not worth all this happening. But I see you have a lot to bear yourself, so I'm releasing you. Don't leave the county. I have no idea to what extent this case will go or what the prosecuting attorney will do, or even if he'll expect you to testify. But I'll send word to your husband you're free on house arrest and he can come get you."

She nodded. "I pray a lot for forgiveness."

Dell grasped her shoulder and left the room. He sent word with a boy who had a horse to go tell Buster his wife could go home.

He and Lake went to lunch at the saloon. The sideboard lunch was a good spread, and they took a table in back to talk, washing down ham sandwiches on rye with cold beer.

"How in the hell did you ever get her to admit all that?"

"Hiram, Angel said he used her body before he left, and I suspect he needed it often by the tone of her voice. If he did that, he might have assaulted Rachel too. And he did."

"I wonder what other alias this Rollo uses. Surely the Rangers have run into him before. I'm waiting for a wire to come through."

"I bet they know about him. She said that the old man went out to El Paso to hire them to break his grandsons out of jail."

A young man came up to the table. "Sheriff, Wilbur says when you finish lunch to meet him at the funeral home."

"What is it?"

"Charles Cody is dead."

"How did that happen?"

"He said it was a gunfight."

Dell paid him a quarter. "Thanks. We can eat on the way."

Lake downed the last of his beer. "You thought he might be a problem."

"Obviously he became one. Damn, I should've been there."

"No, Wilbur and Alan are both good lawmen. They did what they had to do."

"You're probably right," Dell agreed, heading for the door. "I hate all this killing, though. And we aren't any closer to getting the ones in question."

"Probably so."

"Well, no one promised me an easy job here. But it sure has mushroomed into a big one this week."

Wilbur and Smith met them at the funeral home porch.

"Dell, we tried to get him to give up and

come in, but he told us hell no and started shooting. There wasn't anything else we could do."

Smith nodded, grim-faced. "It was kill or be killed."

"I'm sorry, boys. I should've gone with you, but I probably couldn't talk him out of it, either."

The ranger shook his head. "No, Dell. He just flat was not going to be arrested."

"Wilbur, you need to find Billy Lee and fill out the details for him to rule on. Doc needs to look at the body, too."

"We already sent for Doc."

"You two had lunch?"

"Haven't had the chance," Wilbur replied.

"Go on down to the saloon and get some lunch off the board. Doc won't need you. We had a breakthrough with Missus Combs this morning." He looked over his shoulder, checking around to be certain no one was close enough to hear. "Rollo stayed three days at her house planning the robbery. She also said Robert knew the boys well enough. They knew he was underpaid and might help for a share. The family used the money they withdrew to pay the outlaws for the jailbreak."

"What got her to talking?" Wilbur asked.

Lake chuckled. "Dell found a soft spot

she didn't want revealed and she told us all she knew."

"I can tell you the whole story later in privacy. It all makes sense now, though, and we'll figure out what to do next."

Wilbur nodded. "We'll get lunch and meet you at the jail afterward."

Dell agreed. He and Lake headed back to his office at the jail, only to find a wire waiting for them on the desk.

Party you seek is a well-liked business-man who owns some saloons and gro-cery stores in El Paso. He is highly-respected and serves on several boards and committees. Are you certain he was involved in the crime you describe? We have no word on his involvement in any criminal activity in this region, but we will investigate.

Captain Hal Brooks

"Well, he must play two parts, huh?" Lake said after reading the wire.

"I'd say from what Rachel and Angel told us, he doesn't have much respect for women, either." Dell shook his head. "We have no other names but his, so we need more information."

"What about this cashier?"

"I suspect he headed west for parts unknown."

"He's up on the wanted list now," Lake said. "We'll get him."

"Too late for us to do any good, too."

Andy came in to report that Mrs. Combs's husband had come and picked her up a half hour earlier.

Lake chuckled. "You mean she missed the news her brother was shot resisting arrest this morning?"

"She'll hear about it soon enough."

"I'd have liked to seen how she took it."

"In the morning we're going after the old man — don't tell a soul."

"I won't," Andy said. "But he's liable to fight you too."

"He can come feet-first for my money. He started all this hell to get his guilty grandsons out of jail. I have no concern for what he thinks or wants."

They all agreed on that. Dell filled Wilbur and Smith in on what Rachel had told them, and that rounded out the day.

He walked to his house late in the afternoon, thanking God that his woman was there waiting for him when he stepped inside the front door.

"I heard you sent Missus Combs home today. Did she tell you what she knew?"

Dell shook his head warily. "That and more. It was a sorry story." He hugged and kissed her. "I'll tell you all about it."

He explained about Rachel Combs's confession and Guinn shook her head. "That was the horrible price she paid. I mean, it doesn't justify the murders, but what a tough deal. You say that man Magnus is highly respected in El Paso?"

"I bet the Rangers find a bunch of things they never knew about him before."

"And the cashier was a friend of the brothers?"

"Rachel said they knew he didn't make much money at the bank and would be interested in a share of the robbery. She also thought he had the information to open the vault. But if he did, there'd be witnesses. That may well be the reason they killed everyone."

"So what happens next?"

"We arrest the old man in the morning."

"Will he fight that?"

"I imagine he will."

"You be careful. They might make a last stand out there."

"We will. You doing all right?"

"I'm doing fine. This sneaking around is inconvenient, but it's better than not being with you. I hope the judge in Waco can help us."

"Amen. Let's eat this lovely supper you prepared."

"I'm not complaining about our affair, but it would be better, I think, if we were married."

"I'm doing all I can."

She reached across the table and squeezed his hand. "I know that."

"It will come. I promise."

The posse rode out before dawn and arrived as the sky in the east grew rosy. Seated on his horse in the cedars, waiting as the other men surrounded the ranch headquarters, Dell could smell the hog pens. The sour aroma was close to breathtaking. The dogs were barking and would warn the residents, but they'd have to decide to surrender or meet the consequences.

He pushed the horse in closer and held the rifle in his hands. Gunshots didn't panic the animal. Time to dry his palm on the trigger hand and be ready for whatever would explode.

Someone come out the front door arms held high. It was Ira Cody, the old man himself. "I give up. Don't shoot."

Dell raised the rifle. "I have you in my sights. You make one wrong move, and I'll drill you with this here rifle."

"I said I surrender, didn't I? I ain't got a gun on me."

"Handcuff him, Wilbur."

"I have that handled." His deputy hurried up the steps and handcuffed the old man while the other officers covered him. Dell booted his horse closer.

"You're being arrested for your involvement in the robbery and murders."

"I have an alibi."

Dell shook his head. "We have enough witnesses to tie you to the crime. Have someone saddle you a horse. They can pick it up later at the livery."

"You can talk to my lawyer, I'm not saying a thing. You won't be the sheriff after we have elections, Dell Hoffman."

"You going to run against me?"

"No, but there'll be better man than you in that office next term."

"Good. He may improve the jail for your prison term before they take you to Huntsville."

"This would never have happened if you'd minded your own business. That SOB they shot needed killing. He was worthless."

"Put him on a horse. I've heard enough." Dell warily looked around at the shabbily-dressed women now clustered on the porch crying. Some were Ira's daughters. Another was the woman that folks around town said was his wife, while others were his concubines that lived here with them.

He recalled Tilly's comments about his gray head.

Dell reined his horse around and shook his head. They were ready to leave. The old man better have a last look at this place. At his age he might never get back here.

They arrived back in town and drew a crowd at the jail.

Smith took Dell aside. "Rachel Combs hung herself last night."

"Damn. We'll get blamed for that, won't we?"

"Safe bet," the Ranger agreed.

Dell found a letter on his desk. It had been mailed from nearby Forest Hill, Texas. It was hand-printed and had several misspelled words.

To Shariff Huufman.
I know ware that slizzy casher Robert is at. He got a girl near San Antonio named Faye Tomas. U finds her and U got him.

A worried man

Smith laughed. "How near San Antonio?

That would be a needle in haystack to find her."

"Get a notice out. Someone might know her as Faye Thomas, too. There's a chance he may end up there."

"I'll do that," Lake said. "It's our only lead of the day."

"Piece by piece, we gather things like trying to glue a broken plate back together."

Wilbur came in holding a report. "Someone stole five horses from the KTK Ranch yesterday and headed south."

"How many rustlers?" Dell went to the big map of West Texas tacked to the wall of his office. "Wire the law in these three counties with a description of the horse brands. One of them will get them."

"Law enforcement is getting a lot easier," Smith said. "I like it this way."

An older man stopped in later and told them he thought those bank robbers from Dallas he wanted were up at a hangout for trash on Conejos Creek. Dell thanked him and told Wilbur he needed to go home and get some rest. They'd go check out the camp about dawn. Smith volunteered to go with them. Lake planned to sleep in and check on any wires that came in for them.

Guinn shook her head when he arrived home early to report he was going after the bank robbers up on the creek.

"You sure are getting lots of horse riding in. No problems this morning?"

"No, he surrendered. There were several women there. I understand he has daughters, but I suspect some other women there are his other wives."

"He a polygamist?' she asked with a sly grin.

"I have no idea, but there sure are some funny things going on up there."

"You see any you wanted?"

"You rascal, they reminded me of the bad pig smell that hung in the air."

She shook her head. "That's horrible."

"That's what I thought." He hugged and kissed her.

"Oh, Grandpa Cody threatened me with there being a new sheriff in charge next election."

"What can he do about that?"

"I hope from prison they don't count his vote."

"Missus Combs hung herself?"

"Yes. I am glad she didn't do it in my jail. She was very upset about the entire deal. But if I could have stopped it, I would have. Her brother did the same fighting Wilbur and Alan Smith. Best of the day was a letter saying the cashier Robert was at his girlfriend's place outside of San Antonio."

"Where?"

"Just San Antonio. Nothing more specific."

"What next?"

"The Dallas bank robbers. Wilbur, Alan, and I will be up there when the sun comes up."

"Supper's ready. I'll set the alarm and I am happy to share you."

"You're great. Someday it will be different."

"Don't worry about me. I'm here till you run me off."

"No chance of that happening." He buttered a freshly-made sourdough roll. A big bite and the saliva flooded his mouth. He damn sure wasn't going to lose her.

Early the next morning after breakfast, he joined the others and they rode south for the place he hoped to find the two Dallas bank robbers. Why had those two not left the country? Why, he'd have pedaled his way to Mexico any way he could have by this time if he'd got busted out of jail.

No telling about why folks do things. Those two got less than four hundred dollars out of their bank robbery. According to reports, the tellers gave them bags of coins instead of paper money, claiming that was all they had. They dropped several of them escaping or the bags busted. It showed crime didn't pay, and dumb people shouldn't engage in such things in the first place. Maybe they could find them hiding out. They'd gone to see some Mexican *puta* to borrow money. Heavens, how much money could she have had to spare working in that other sorry camp? Pitiful deal.

But he'd bet the man from El Paso had earned well over twenty thousand dollars from the robbery of Thompson's bank. Probably kept half of it for himself.

And why did Robert participate in the deal? Little dumb mousey guy in his thirties who'd had an ongoing affair with Angel he had never known about. Be lucky this Rollo guy didn't cut his throat, too and leave him for dead out in West Texas. The 'respected citizen' role in El Paso still had him wondering what exactly 'respect' meant in that far corner of Texas.

They rode all day and arrived about dark. He hated that they were so late finding this camp and that none of them knew the layout. Another rag-tag deal like the others for losers sprawled out in a canyon of cedar and live oak. It had a central hand pump and place to water your horse, wash clothes, or take a bath, but that was about it.

A young woman was bathing in the tank and Alan Smith rode up and asked if she knew some men named Arnold Hale or Dale Kempt. In the last rays of sundown, all she had on standing beside the large trough was her thin wet skirt. She stopped washing herself with a wet rag.

"You like what you see?"

"Right now, I'd like to see them."

"You like men more than women, huh?"

"Not that way. I need to talk to them."

"Well how much is it worth to show you them?"

"Ten *pesos.*"

"Crazy man. I wouldn't ask you that much to let you use my body." She threw down the rag, gathered her skirt and waved him on. They dismounted. Wilbur held the horses. Dell, Lake, and Smith followed the wet tart up the hill in the fading light to a tent under some trees.

"They're both passed out drunk in that tent. Pay me ten pesos." She held out her hand.

Smith went in his pocket, but Dell beat him to it and dropped the money in her hand.

"Now you have them. Who wants me?"

"Ma'am," Dell said, "we're Rangers and came to arrest these two men for bank robbery, escaping jail, and horse thieving."

"Well, I'll have you know I've been to bed with a Ranger before."

The three went to laughing. Smith said, "I bet you have, and if I wasn't on official business right now, ma'am, you could have my business. Do they have those horses they stole?"

"No. They sold them two days ago for money to get drunk on."

"It lasted this long — the drink?"

"I think they finished it this afternoon."

"Is there anyone has a wagon we can hire to haul them to my jail in Thomas City?"

"I bet Scroggins would do that for ten bucks."

"Where is he?"

She looked hard at Smith. "Well he's down in camp. I can find him for you — for a fee."

"How much?"

"Two *pesos,* I guess?"

"I have the money," Dell assured her. "You lead the way. Alan, Hiram, you two can drag the prisoners downhill to load them."

She took him to the old man with the scattered whiskers and corncob pipe. "Whatcha need?" he asked Dell.

"Two prisoners hauled back to Thomas

City. What do you charge?"

"I told him ten bucks," she said.

"I can do that for that. You coming along darling?"

"If you like me to, since I'm rich tonight. I may find a new dress to wear over there."

Dell had his doubts she ever wore much of anything, but paid her the two dollars.

The old man harnessed his team and the Rangers delivered the two drunk, hand-cuffed, stumbling cowboys ready to load. The dead-drunk felons were piled in on the bare boards. Wilbur brought the lawmen their horses.

The brazen hussy turned her nose up about going along, but stayed to do so once Smith showed back up. Lake led the way. Dell and Wilbur followed the wagon. Smith said he'd join them later.

The creaky old wagon needed axle grease. The old horses could hardly walk, let alone trot. Dell left Wilbur in charge while he and Lake took off for town. They figured they wouldn't see Smith again until morning.

Dell watered and unsaddled his horse and put him in the barn with access to the pad-dock in the back. It still wasn't dawn when he staggered inside and removed his boots.

Guinn came down the stairs to meet him. "Dell! Did you just get back?"

115

"I'm dead tired." He sat on the kitchen chair and mopped his face in his hands.

"You want breakfast?"

"No, sleep. We got those two. Had no problem, but the story is damn funny. I'll tell you later how it went."

She hugged his head to her bosom. "I'm just glad you're back safe, big man. Get some sleep. I'll be here waiting when you wake up."

"Good." They went upstairs. He shucked his clothes off in the floor, kissed her one last time, and dozed off.

Groggy-headed when he awoke, he saw it was almost sundown. He dressed and came down the stairs, finding Guinn in the kitchen.

"Get some rest?"

"I don't think so. This business is about to get me down. Those worthless bank robbers sold the damn horses they stole to get drunk and were passed out in some makeshift tent up there. I had to hire a old man and his beat-up wagon to bring them back. That isn't the worst. Some half-dressed dove showed us where they were for a fee."

"She did what?"

"It was dark. All we wanted were those two. She was bathing in a horse tank and for ten pesos, she showed us where they were. What a mess." They both were laughing. "I've been working as a lawman for fifteen years. Solving crimes, trailing down killers and robbers day in and day out. But this has to be the most difficult job I've ever have been involved in. And I'm getting nowhere."

"Not so. You only lack two prisoners now who escaped."

"The prime ones. The Cody brothers."

"Exactly. You have the crime planner in jail — the old man. You only lack Robert and the men involved in the crime."

"He may be the only outsider who knows them beside Rollo."

"Yes, they killed the rest," she said softly. "What next?"

"I need to find Robert. They say he's with a woman down there."

"How will you find him?"

"Circle the town. If she's a dove, someone will recall her. Then I can run him down."

"Can Wilbur handle the business here?"

"Yes."

"If they found this man Rollo had done anything illegal in El Paso, wouldn't the Rangers out there have told you?"

"I thought that they'd uncovered it by now."

"How did Old Man Cody find him out

117

there if he was such a sterling citizen?"

"Good question. I'll ask him tomorrow."

"Will he answer you?"

He never said a word, merely nodded his head. That old sumbitch would tell him all he knew about Rollo in the morning. If there was any secret that old bastard knew, he'd better spill it or he'd drown before lunch.

Dell went down to the store and secured a tin bathtub before they closed. He told the clerk he only wanted to borrow it for a day, not buy it. Then he had it carried over to the jail and told the night jailer where to set it in the middle of the room and to have it filled three-quarters full that evening by a prisoner or two. That set, he walked back home.

Kissing his fiancée when she met him at the door, he whispered, "More honeymoon time."

And they did.

Afterwards, lying side-by-side holding hands in the dark bedroom, he said softly, "I can tell you discovered something tonight when we talked."

"You are getting to be fortune teller?"

"No I am going to get him to talk today."

He rolled over and kissed her. "I will share it tomorrow night with you."

"Good. You sound better."

I may even be better tomorrow night.

SEVEN

First thing next morning, Dell stopped by the blacksmith shop and spoke to Sam Hampton, the strongest man in town.

"How you doing Dell?"

He got straight to the point. "Not good, Sam. I still have multiple questions I need answered about the murders and robbery. I have a man knows the outfit who did it all, but he won't tell me a thing. But if someone held his head underwater long enough, I think I'd learn all he knows."

"What can I do to help you?"

"Hold him in the dunking tank till he tells us what we need to know."

"How big is he?"

"Not near as big as you, hoss."

"When do you need me?"

"Nine o'clock this morning."

"At the jail?"

Dell nodded. "Right. I won't take long."

"Whatever helps you solve that crime."

"Not a word outside the jail, though."

"No problem for me."

"That's why I came to talk to you."

"See you at nine o'clock."

"Thanks."

Dell went on to the jail. He found Wilbur Caine waiting for him, curious about the appearance of the tub.

"Who's taking a bath?" the deputy asked.

"Put out a kitchen chair and get the old man in here. Today he's telling us all he knows."

Wilbur chuckled. "Maybe cuss us out some more."

"No, he's going to answer us. Sam Hampton's going to help you drown him in the tub. I've had enough."

Wilbur nodded, setting down the chair out for the man to sit in. "I think them Rangers call it going swimming, huh?"

"Something like that. Handcuff him behind his back. It'll be easier that way."

"You think he knows all about it?"

"Ira's the one went to El Paso and found this Rollo character. Then he hired him and they met at Rachel's house to plan things. I want a list of the men rode in here with Rollo and murdered those people." Dell's voice hardened. "At any cost."

"I agree. Time to get him?"

"Yes. Let him sit uncomfortable."

The old man looked rough, with his several days' growth of beard on his chin. His language was all cuss words, but not one of them was fresh or new.

Dell set another chair across from the prisoner, so the tub of water would be between them. "Today, Ira, I want the full story about your first trip to El Paso after the jury found your grandsons guilty of murder. I want the whole story and nothing left out. No part not told to us."

"You can go straight to —"

He shut the sputtering old man up with a backhanded slap across the face. "I've about had enough of your mouth."

The front door opened behind him. Dell looked over his shoulder and watched Sam Hampton enter.

"Well, hello, Sam. Have a seat. I was just telling Mister Cody I wanted the whole story about his visit to El Paso after his grandsons' murder trial." He turned back to the shackled prisoner. "Ira, you see this tub?"

"Yeah. What about it?"

"Sam and Wilbur think a bath may help you recover your memory about El Paso. I'll caution you, though, that I don't give a damn if you drown taking a bath in my jail.

So what'll it be?"

"Go to hell. I ain't telling you anything."

"Have it your way." Dell shrugged, crossed his legs and folded his arms. "Hold him under until the bubbles stop, boys."

Ira proved no problem for the two men to lift and douse belly down over the tub. He did lots of protesting, kicking his feet like a paddle boat, but Hampton's powerful grip on his neck kept him submerged easily. When he grew quiet, Dell waved for them to bring him up.

Vomiting water, Ira was still fighting mad.

"Mister Cody, I'm dead serious about this matter. Are you ready to talk to me about that trip?"

"Fuck no!"

He gave the down signal and back under the water he went. This time he stomped his feet.

They let him up.

"I'm going to kill you," he screamed between coughs.

Dell was not impressed. "That'd be a trick after you're drowned, wouldn't it? Back in the water, boys."

"No. No. I'll tell you the whole thing."

"No games. No tricks."

Ira hacked up a mouthful of water and spat, tried to catch his breath. "No. Just don't dunk me again."

Dell nodded for the boys to let him go. Sam and Wilbur set Ira up straight in the chair. His shirt was soaked and there was a big puddle on the floor. Water drained from his too-long grey hair and off his beard. His eyes were red and wide with fear, and he was trembling like a leaf.

"Start with why you went to El Paso."

"Oh, hell. You've about killed me, you bastards."

"Ira, if you don't tell me everything, I *will* kill you. And no one but your little harem would miss you."

The old man nodded that he understood. "I had to do something. Them boys were supposed to carry our family on. They were good boys. I couldn't see them hang."

Dell rolled his eyes, but held his tongue. "Go on."

"I was desperate. Someone told me there were people in El Paso that would do anything for enough money. So I got on the stage and went over there." He erupted in another coughing fit, this time bringing up more than water. Ira puked between his knees, unable to move with his hands cuffed behind his back. The smell was sickening. Dell tried to ignore it but it stung his nose.

"Who told you about these guys?"

"Ah, Freddy Warren. He lived out there for a few years."

"What name did he give you?"

"Rollo Magnus."

"Did you know he was a businessman?"

Ira nodded. "Freddy said he had lots of business, some legal, some illegal. Said Magnus got lots of whorehouse girls from Mexico to work in the states, and shipped several American girls from here to Mexico City. He said a good-looking blonde girl was worth as much as ten thousand dollars at fourteen to sixteen years old."

"You didn't go there to sell a teen slave, did you?"

"No. God, no. Magnus wouldn't even talk to me at first. He thought I was a Pinkerton or something. So I sent him a newspaper with the story about my boys in it, along with a letter saying I needed them out of jail at any cost. That I'd pay anything for his help."

"Then what happened?"

"A lawyer called on me at my hotel. He took me across the border in Juarez and quizzed me for two hours with some tough *hombres* standing over me. He told me I had to pay two thousand dollars just to meet Magnus. I agreed, but I said I'd only pay it to him. Not his greaser lawyer." Ira laughed once. "That pissed him off, but I stayed tough. He finally said Magnus would only meet me at his ranch by Mesilla."

"And you met him there?"

"Yes. But he wanted five thousand to even consider getting the boys out. I didn't have the money. So he asked if there was a bank where I lived. I said yes. He asked if 'n it could be robbed while they freed the boys. I said I had no idea. Hell, I never robbed a bank. He asked how much money was in it? I said I'd find out. I knew Robert was always short on money, and would tell me what I needed to know for a price. So Magnus and me shook hands. I paid him two thousand dollars, and he corresponded with Rachel. She never opened one of the letters, just passed them on to me."

"How was Robert in the deal?" Dell asked.

"I paid him five hundred dollars to help them if needed. He'd open the safe if Thompson wouldn't. If there was over ten thousand in the bank when they robbed it, Magnus said he'd pay him fifteen hundred."

"Was he at the bank when they robbed it?'

Ira nodded. "They had to be sure the safe was opened."

"Who killed the family and raped the women?"

"I don't know that."

"Ira, you know everything. Tell me who got left with the family. Who did the killing?"

"That was not in my deal. He had five men back from El Paso way. Meanest, fiercest men I ever met. Three stayed at the house. They took a fancy to the Thompson girl and talked about taking her to Mexico and selling her as a slave. Magnus told them no — too far to go to conceal her. She might get away and expose them."

"What was those men's names left at the house?"

Ira looked at the floor. "Pedro Paulus. Monte Garcia, Hidalgo Andre."

Wilbur wrote down the names.

"They all live in Mexico?"

"Most of the time, I guess."

"Who was at the bank?"

"Magnus, Robert, and a man they called Sanchez."

"And the jail?"

"Phillip Snyder — he wasn't a Mexican like the others."

"Meanwhile, those first three murdered and raped the Thompsons?"

"They were only supposed to guard them."

Enraged, Dell jumped up and grabbed the

old man by the shirt, shaking him hard. "They planned to kill and rape them. They weren't going to leave a witness in the damn town. I know it and you know it."

"I had no gawdamn part of that —"

"Bullshit you didn't. You hired those killers, you lying bastard."

"All I wanted was my grandsons out of your gawdamn jail."

"You knew that bastard Rollo raped Rachel every night he stayed at her house. Drove her to suicide. Were those boys worth that? Your own daughter? Were they really worth that?"

"I only heard that later after you arrested her."

"Where are the boys now?"

"Down in Mexico, where you can't touch 'em."

This drew an angry laugh from Dell. "Ira, I have no intention of bringing them back here. I intend to leave them for buzzards to eat. They aren't worth bringing home."

"You —"

"Wilbur, put this sorry excuse for a man back in his cell. I can't stand the sight of him."

"Yes, sir." With rough hands, the deputy yanked Ira up from the chair and shoved him back toward the cells.

Dell turned to Hampton. "Sam, thank you. I am sorry you had to endure such sorry proceedings."

The big man nodded. "Like I said, Dell. Anything I can do to help you close this thing."

They shook hands and Hampton left, headed back to the smithy. Dell sat back down and thought about what came next. Wilbur found him there after coming back from the cell block.

"You okay, Dell?"

He shook his head. "Not even close, son."

"Where do we go from here?"

Dell came to a decision. Looking up at the younger man, he sighed. "I'm going home. I have to tell a wonderful woman I must leave her to go find these scum. As for you . . . Wilbur, I appoint you to be the sheriff until I return. If I'm killed, Guinn Howard is to have my earthly things."

"You're going — alone?"

"I need you here. Find a good man to take your place. Tell the Marshal I'll be packing to go and we can talk this afternoon. I need to tell the woman I love my plans next. Wilbur, no matter what happens, you be sure Ira Cody is tried for his crimes. And any other with a part in them."

His man looked to be sick over his decision. "One man against an army? You can't go alone."

"I'll be fine."

Wilbur was close to tears. Dell hugged him manly-like and told him to buck up. He had a big job ahead.

"I know that, Dell. I just don't know if I can fill your boots."

The walk to his house was even longer.

"Why do you look so down?" Guinn asked when she saw him come through the door.

"Let's sit in the living room," he said. "I have to tell you something sad."

"What is it?"

"Ira Cody spilled his guts. I know the names of the killers now, and they're in far-off places. It's my sworn duty to uphold the laws of Texas and solve the crimes in my county. Since the Rangers can't find them, I'm going out there to arrest them. If I arrest them, the Rangers will be obligated to get them back here by relay to stand trial. They've always done it that way. But I may be gone for a long time, and I hate that for both of us. This won't be any small round trip to arrest someone and come home. It'll be hardest on you. I plan to marry you when we get your divorce final, but I can't tell you when I'll return."

"Dell, I will be here when you do. I can't

130

stand the thought that they may kill you and I'll never know what happened to you. But I also know you well enough that you'll come back for me when that job is over." She began to cry. "I understand your need to do this. I know you would never be happy until they're all behind bars."

He held her in his arms and felt sick to his stomach to have her crying on him. Her tears soaked into his shirt. This might be the dumbest thing he ever did in his entire life — but he would never be able to live with himself if he didn't catch these animals. What they'd done had been pure evil, the work of the devil. Justice for the Thompson family had to be served.

"I've saved some money and didn't keep it in the bank. I don't know why, but my daddy lost money twice when banks failed. So while I had a few hundred dollars in Thompson's Bank, I have eight hundred dollars saved here. I'm going to leave you six hundred to live on, and if I need more, I'll call upon you to wire some to me."

"No, you should take at least three hundred. I can sew it into your vest tonight so you have enough. If you'll let me stay in your house, I can live on five hundred for two years or more. I hope by then you will return safely. If you need money, I can wire it to you."

"I made that money off cattle drives I took to Kansas. Wanted to buy a ranch, but never did. So I built the house here, instead."

"I'm very proud of this house. And I'll be proud to live here with you."

"I'm making a will. The house will be yours if I don't make it back."

"Oh, Dell, what will I do if you don't?"

"I'm going to try to be careful as I can be. But you know the dangers of law work. Take good care of yourself so we can still have a good life when this is over."

"I won't try to talk you out of going. I know you, and how you get when you make your mind up — you go on and do it. Just remember, I will be here for you."

His leaving took two days. The liveryman, Robert Perlman, gave him a sound pack-horse that led easy. He also wouldn't take any money for it. The town's business folk took it upon themselves to oufit him, providing everything from a bedroll, to food, to a sturdy pack. The store man gave him an oilskin slicker in case of rain. A rancher friend gave him a good packsaddle outfit and a small tent. He had two tin plates and cups, a small pot, a coffee pot, a grill to cook on, a small skillet, an ax, and a bow saw. He secured a new canvas sheet to cover his pack and extra ropes, along with three pairs of handcuffs. Along with food supplies, his packhorse would be loaded.

When it came to weapons, Dell decided to take all three of his revolvers — his short-barrel, Sheriff's model .45, another good single action .45 the town saddlemaker fixed a holster for on the fork of his saddle, and a small .30 caliber Colt in his boot. To this he added his Winchester rifle in its saddle scabbard, and two knives to use for defense or cutting.

Last, but certainly not least, he carried in his pockets several John Doe warrants and search warrants from Billy Lee.

Folks came by to thank him when they got word, bringing more cakes and cookies than he could pack. Still sick over his decision, he slept with Guinn the last night and as the last stars shone in the cold sky overhead they loaded the pack horse and saddled Burt. After one long last kiss and more than a few tears, he rode west as the first rays of dawn broke over the horizon.

Dell made forty miles the first day, avoiding towns and any watching eyes that could warn the outlaws of his coming. But on the third day, he hit the El Paso stage line road. Things turned drier, but stage stops every twenty miles or so to feed and water the horses made his trip move on at a good pace.

He wrote Guinn from Big Springs, three days out of El Paso. He didn't have much to say, but he missed her, so he talked about the horses. They were doing all right because he grained them and they acted even better than when he first rode them out on the corn or oats he'd brought with him. He made sure their backs were clean and the saddle pads were, too. He told her that he'd taken to calling the packhorse Rod, and he was proud of him as he was of Burt, his prized Steel Dust gelding. He also found himself talking more to his horses in the absence of company. He talked to them about everything, even the weather.

Out of Big Springs, he entered the Rio Grande valley and rode by the irrigated farms bordering the river. Grapes, citrus, beans, and corn grew in the fields. Two or three had cotton planted. Everywhere he saw adobe *jacals.* Some were *haciendas,* others burro outfits. Many friendly Mexican women in colorful dresses under straw hats walked the dusty road to and from small stores in the towns. Many smiled and waved at him or their children shouted, *"A vaquero, mamacita!"*

Dell just tipped his hat and moved on.

After eight days, he finally made El Paso. He put the horses in a livery, took a bath, had his clothes washed and ironed by a Chinese woman at the bath house, and ate a big cooked meal of Mexican food in a restaurant. The only thing he didn't enjoy was the beer. It was cool, not cold. They had no ice.

The next day, he went to the local Ranger headquarters. He met Captain Hal Brooks who'd written him the telegram about Rollo Magnus. Brooks was a big man, with salt-and-pepper hair and drooping mustaches. He was nice enough as they visited, but Dell kept what he knew about Magnus to himself. If he pushed for Rollo's arrest, it would be big news down here, and the others would likely run for the hills.

"We have examined *Señor* Magnus's business dealings here in El Paso," Brooks told him. "He's a prominent citizen and we found nothing suspicious."

Dell shrugged. "Well, I guess I was wrong. Strange to me that his name came up from witnesses."

"Oh, he may be an outlaw, just not here. But it does beg the question — just why are you here, Sheriff Hoffman?"

"I have a prisoner at home that gave me the list of the men who robbed the bank and murdered those five people in my county seat. They also let all my jailed prisoners out — including two other murderers."

"What are the names? I may know them if they come from around here."

"Pedro Paulus."

Brooks grunted. "He's a border outlaw, and a nasty one. I have a warrant for his arrest if he ever shows up here. Mexico won't arrest and send them across. Paulus is a fast gunman. He's killed several men, all, he claims, in self-defense, which is easy out here if the man shot wears a gun. You think he rode clear up there to rob a bank?"

"They were paid to get those two killers out of jail," he replied. "Several thousand dollars apiece, as I understand it, and that's not even talking about the proceeds from the bank robbery."

"I see. Who else?"

"Monte Garcia."

"Another man from Juarez I have a warrant for."

"Hidalgo Andre."

"I want him too."

"Does a man named Sanchez run with them?"

"No doubt. This is a common border name. It could be Alfredo Sanchez. He's another tough *hombre*."

"How about Phillip Snyder from Mesilla?"

"Hmm. What did he do up there?"

"He let the prisoners out and gave the Cody brothers their horses. Why?"

"My man Curley Thomas is on his trail about his dealings in the white slave business. Thomas will be in here this evening. Snyder won't be hard to arrest. He runs a hotel, bar, and café here. Gambler, too. Now I can see him as a possible slaver of women. Curley had some information on him. We hear about such deals, but they are slick and over the border before we can act. Who told you about him?"

"The grandfather who paid them to get his grandsons out."

"How did he find all these men?"

"When the jury found his grandsons guilty, he knew they couldn't bust them out of my jail — I'd have caught them and planned to hang them, too. But the old man heard about a guy down here that will do just about anything if the price is right. So he came and paid two thousand dollars just to talk to the man."

"That's lots of money just to talk to someone. Who did two grand buy him an audience with?"

"Rollo Magnus."

Brooks shook his head. "I bet he's never been in that country."

"How much?"

"Pardon me?" The Ranger looked confused.

"How much will you bet?"

"You're serious."

He nodded. "The owner of my town's saloon identified a man with a large burn scar on his right cheek. Told me he walked in one day and asked where to find a particular whore in my town. When I talked to her, she backed the story up. The man with the scar's name was Rollo Magnus, she said, and he used her crib for a meeting with the bank teller, who was also one of her regular clients. I found out later that Magnus was staying with the daughter of the man who hired him, Ira Cody. He stayed three days making plans for the bank robbery and jailbreak by day, and raping her every night."

"My Lord." Brooks squirmed in his chair, looking uncomfortable. "Maybe — maybe we haven't looked at him closely enough yet."

"I don't want him messed with until I have his outfit all rounded up. My witness swore under oath that Rollo sold Mexican girls to American whorehouses all the time. He's also supposed to sell blonde teenage

138

American girls in Mexico City for several thousand dollars apiece."

"That's heard often on the wind down here, but so far we haven't caught them with girls in their possession. Now we have names we can check out."

"If we can get one guy and twist his ear, we might tie more into it," Dell agreed.

"Who paid your expenses to come down here?"

"I paid my own."

"Damn." Brooks looked shocked at the answer. "You're determined."

"I take my job seriously, Captain. They killed a family. I discovered their bodies. Bloodiest murder scene I ever saw or heard about. Ira Cody testified they considered taking Thompson's teenage daughter to Mexico to sell her, but Rollo said she'd be too hard to conceal over that distance."

"So they raped and murdered her instead."

"That's about the size of it."

"I understand now why you made the trip." Brooks beat a lead pencil on the desk like drum stick. "Damn, that bastard must be slick."

"Magnus? He must be. He planned the thing down to the second, and then they were gone." Dell blew in his open hand.

"Like smoke."

"Where do you think we should start?"

"The weak link. This Snyder feller sounds like he has the most to lose."

The Ranger smiled. "I like the way you think."

That evening Dell, Curley Thomas, and Captain Brooks had a fine private meal with a Mexican woman named Juanita. During the meal, she told Dell to bring his horses to her, that she would charge him half the price the livery charged. Brooks and Thomas assured him she was honest and on the level, and a trusted *amigo.* He agreed. Then things turned to more pressing business.

Dell told his whole story to Curley Thomas, a blond boy barely old enough to shave, yet walked with the swagger of a seasoned lawman. The young Ranger had been after Snyder over the slaving business for a year, but had simply never found enough evidence of his involvement to arrest him. Brooks asked if they could send someone in undercover as a buyer and trip Snyder up in his own web.

"Who would we send?" Thomas wanted to know.

"Why, that's easy." Dell smiled. "Me, of course."

EIGHT

Philip Snyder owned a large hotel and saloon called the Eagle's Nest in Mesilla. Stepping off the stage from El Paso, Dell felt a wave of disgust wash over him at the sheer glitter of the joint. What kind of men would feel the need to rape, murder, and pillage good folk when they had this to come home to?

Bastards.

Clamping down on the feeling, he took a deep breath and stalked up the hotel's front steps. At the front desk, he checked in under the name John White, the alias he, Thomas, and Brooks had agreed upon while planning this caper. After dropping his bags off in his room, he headed downstairs to the saloon. There he found Snyder, holding court at the bar.

"Well, well, another newcomer," he said in a voice as slick as his hair. "What's your name, sir?"

Dell relaxed slightly. He felt certain he had never seen this man in the white shirt and tie. "John White. From up Dallas way."

"Philip Snyder, your host." They shook hands. "What's your poison, Mister White?"

"Whisky," Dell said. "Neat."

"A man who knows what he wants. I like that." Snyder called over the bartender, a fancy dan in a vest and tie. "Turner, a glass of the top-shelf whisky. Make it a double." Obviously, the man was a show-off.

"Coming right up, Mister Snyder."

They stood at the bar, drinking whiskey and making small talk. For a while, Dell wondered if he'd ever get the opening he'd need to talk business. But Snyder proved to be the curious sort and finally asked him what it was he did in Dallas.

"Nothing," he whispered with a big smile that told the world how proud he was of the fact. "My old lady's got a cathouse. She makes the living. I just spend her money."

Spencer laughed. "Aw, you're kidding me?"

"Naw, she sent me down here —" He stopped and made sure no one was in earshot. "You know, to find her some girls to work for her."

"Dumb teenagers?"

"Younger the better," Dell agreed.

"You really want some?"

"Well, if I can afford 'em. Times are tough these days. We ain't making the money we want to. Figured if we can get some cheap ones we can make more money than we do now with white girls, huh?"

"How about four hundred apiece?"

That had gone easily. "How would I ever get 'em back to Dallas?" he asked.

Snyder grinned like a man with all the answers. "I've got a traveling medicine wagon will haul them up there for twenty-five dollars a piece."

Dell went to figuring on his fingers. "That's four twenty-five apiece?"

"I think I can knock off five dollars a head. I have to talk to the boss. But he usually does what I suggest."

"He live close by?"

"Oh yeah. Tomorrow I'll have the deal cut and dried. How do you contact your wife?"

"I telegraph her and act like I'm buying cows. Does she want some new cows for four hundred-twenty bucks a head?"

"Oh, now that's smart." Snyder sniggered. "You've done this before, I take it?"

"Not out here. They say you've got prettier ones out here than they got in Brownsville."

"Oh, yeah."

"When can I check back and find out if I have a deal?"

"Tomorrow evening. Say about five."

"I thank you for your time, Mister Snyder." They shook hands again and finished their drinks before parting ways.

Dell met Curley Thomas after midnight down by the Rio Grande in a cottonwood grove.

"I learned a lot. Snyder has Mexican girls for four hundred dollars a head and a guy with a medicine wagon to haul them to Dallas for twenty bucks apiece."

"A medicine wagon, huh? I always wondered how he got them out of here. Man, you're a top grade spy, Dell. No one I used ever could get him to commit to selling them. Guess your easy ways caught him off guard."

Dell shook his head. "Yeah, who looks in a medicine wagon for white slaves being transported? Smart move."

"Last place I would look. We need to arrange for the money. Captain can get it. Will we see his boss at this deal?"

"I doubt it. He says he handles it all, but has to talk to him about lowering the price for me taking five of them."

"You think he's going to go ask him in El Paso tomorrow?"

"I bet he does."

"We'll have coverage of Magnus. If Snyder shows up, we'll know for sure they're working together like you say."

"Good." Dell felt better about the whole idea. If the connection was made to buy the girls, the Rangers would help him arrest Magnus in the end. That suited him perfectly.

Dell stayed two more nights in the Eagle's Nest Hotel, waiting on the deal to be finalized. He wondered about Guinn and how she was making it. She had been on his mind the entire trip and he felt guilty for leaving her behind at home. But certainly this was no place for her.

Finally, on his third evening in town, he was invited to dinner at Snyder's place.

His man came in a suit and tie then after he made sure they were alone in the booth he said, "I got you the price on them cows you wanted. My drive boss will be here at midnight on Friday to show you the stock. If you approve, he'll head out for Dallas with them."

"I'll have the money here. Unless Wells Fargo goes broke," Dell added with a laugh.

"No chance of that happening. Be in the back alley after midnight. Do you want to test them?"

"I sure want to see they're alive and in one piece."

"We usually get much more than this for them but we want to make you a regular customer, John." Snyder held out his hand in order to seal the deal. Fighting the urge to puke, Dell took it.

Magnus must have really trusted Snyder. Being the only gringo the gang boss brought with him, these two worthless turds were probably thick as cold molasses. They were behind all the murder, rape, and mayhem caused in his small town, and if this deal was any indication, there was no telling what other crimes they'd been involved in. The El Paso businessman and his lackey here were in for a rude awakening in the very near future. It would be the most satisfying arrest he'd ever made when he clamped the cuffs on them.

Finishing his meal, he bid his host good evening and returned to his rooms. At midnight, he slipped out again to meet Curley.

"You were right, Dell," the Ranger reported. "Snyder showed up in Magnus's office in the cafe this morning. No other reason for that meeting. The captain hopes some of those other men you want will be there Friday night at the purchase."

"That would make it a damn sight easier."

Thomas shook his head. "You really think these medicine wagons are how they deliver them?"

"That's what he told me."

"By God, I'm looking inside more of them from now on." The young man laughed. "You ever thought about that before?"

"Hell, no. They come through my town all the time. They won't ever come again, though, that I don't check them out. We had a teenage girl disappear five years ago. Never had any trace of her, but her disappearance might have been hitched to a medicine show passing through."

"You know this is a major breakthrough for us, right?"

"I came a long ways to get these devils. I near vomited when I found the dead family members."

"Just remember that come this Friday evening," Thomas warned him. "They could kill you that quick, too. I should have five Rangers with me. They'll drift into town all through the day. I figure Snyder has several lookouts, and I don't want any of them to be suspicious. Hell will be popping in Mesilla when this takes place, though."

"Let's hope it doesn't get too bad."

"We can handle it, Dell."

147

"Good. I better get back and play some poker."

Later that night around the table, one of the other card players ribbed about not looking at all the whores in the place vying for his attention.

Dell checked his cards and raised the man a quarter. "Hell, back in Dallas I live in a cathouse. My wife runs it and I get all I want free, day or night. These girls here ain't got nothing I want."

The players all laughed. But that settled them down about him not wanting any.

Friday morning, a tall Mexican *pistolero* arrived at the hotel. Sitting at one of the poker tables in the saloon, Dell wondered if the *hombre* was one of the four gunmen he was after, but couldn't risk asking.

Turned out, he didn't need to. A sharp intake of breath came from the man on Dell's right, a teamster named Ule Towers. Dell looked over to find the man's eyes following the newcomer across the floor.

"What's that damn killer Hidalgo Andre doing up here? Must be some bad deal going on." He felt Dell's gaze on him. "You know him, John?"

A shiver went down his spine. Dell shook his head, pretending to be interested in his hand. "Never heard of him."

"He's a hired killer. Meanest sumbitch I ever saw. You better step aside if 'n he comes your way."

He folded. "I'll damn sure do that. I didn't come out here to get killed."

"Neither did I." Towers scowled, and then won the hand.

The realization that he stood to capture two of the men he was after later that evening gave him a thrill. While he had no real fear of either man — Andre or Snyder — he *did* wonder how many more of them would be in on the sale that night, and just how steeply the odds would be stacked against his making it through alive. In the spirit of being prepared, after lunch he sat on a bench in the shade of the saloon's porch and kept his eyes open for the arrival of more obvious *pistoleros*. He didn't have too long to wait.

Another arrived mid-afternoon by buck-board, this one pot bellied and short, sporting a long, shaggy mustache and two pistols on his belt. Dark, wary eyes scanned the porch from under the shade of the wide straw hat he wore, and after a long moment, he started for the *cantina*. As he neared them, a drunk staggered out the batwing door and nearly ran the shorter man over.

"Hey, *amigo,*" he exclaimed. "I didn't see

you there."

The short Mexican caught the drunk by a fistful of his shirt, slammed him into the wall, and drew a wicked-looking knife from a sheath strapped to his leg.

"Watch where you're going, *culo,*" he growled in thickly-accented English. "Or I'll cut your eyes out and feed them to you."

The bleached faced man reeled, holding his Adam's apple protectively. "I'm sorry, Monte. I'll be more careful."

"See that you are," the *pistolero* said.

Monte, Dell thought. *Monte Garcia, I presume?* Damn. That made three of the scorpions on his list present and accounted for so far.

As Garcia passed by him into the *cantina,* a boy scampered up to him on the porch and asked if he was John White. When Dell said that he was, the boy told him a package had arrived for him at the post office, and that he needed to sign for it — probably the money Curley Thomas had promised. Dell thanked him with a quarter, then followed him on down the road.

The thought of the young Ranger's name made him uneasy, though. No way he dared try to warn Thomas and Brooks of the arrival of the outlaws. For all he knew, they had eyes on him right now as he strolled along toward the post office. And while they'd talked about the possibility of the others showing up with Snyder, Dell had no idea how prepared the Rangers really were. Thomas said he should have five men with him. Did that mean he might not?

The package at the post office was exactly what he'd hoped it would be. He signed for it, and returned to the hotel, waiting to open it until he was back in his room. Inside was $2100 in fresh, crisp one-hundred-dollar bills. Dell fanned it out like a card deck, counted it out, and secured it inside his vest pocket. Checking the gun in his boot one last time, he took a deep breath and headed out for supper.

After supper, Dell used the stinking public toilets out back of the hotel. He was seated in one of the stalls taking shallow breaths when he heard two men talking in the booth next door, obviously emptying their bladders.

"This guy is from Dallas?" one of them asked the other.

"He's got a whorehouse there," Snyder's voice answered. "Boss thinks the guy will buy more in the future."

"Sanchez bringing them?"

"Who else?"

He never heard the rest of the conversation as the men exited the privy, but he'd heard enough. *Philip Snyder, Hidalgo Andre, Monte Garcia, and Sanchez* — the only one missing from the to-do tonight would be Pedro Paulus.

Standing up, Dell hitched up his pants. Thank God he wasn't constipated. Catalogue pages were a poor excuse for corncobs.

As he left the privy, though, the term "birds of the feather flock together" made him think more about the coming gathering in the alley at the stroke of midnight. Was it too good to be true, them all being here? This bunch didn't sound suspicious of his role as John White, playboy husband of a Dallas cathouse owner. That cover was the one thing he did not need blown away. If they thought he had the potential to buy more girls in the future, he was not expendable for their business purposes. But they had all hands on deck like in a sea battle he'd read about in a novel.

His entire body itched from the tension. He fought the impulse to fidget and jerk as he walked, and the clock crept along like a snail through molasses. He kept a pocket watch he seldom used because he never needed it with the Texas sun out bright — but today checked it often. He played poker to keep his brain and fingers occupied, even won a few hands. But nothing could keep the pending midnight meeting off his mind. How would it go? Could he and the Rangers ensnare the entire outfit in one roll of the dice? Rangers were a tough fighting force, but the men they faced were some of the meanest around. Most of them knew there was nothing waiting for them but a hanging noose if captured. That would only make them fight harder than a normal person being arrested.

There would be some deaths in that alley when the sun rose in the morning to find them, sure as hell. He didn't want to be the one with his name in the newspaper obituary column.

As the evening wore on, Snyder found him at the poker table. "You ready?"

"Certainly," Dell replied, keeping his tone light.

"You'll be pleased with the ones I have for you. Meet me in my office right after midnight."

He agreed and went to back to his cards.

A new hand was about to be dealt, and a new man sat down across from Dell. He had a tight, thin face, chiseled features, and two gold rings. His suit was tailored, and the white shirt carefully hand-stitched. The narrow-brim Stetson hat he wore was cocked back on his head, and he smoked a long, thick cigar.

But the only thing Dell noticed was the scar on the right side of his hard face.

The cards were dealt, and the first bets made. Dell called the bet and picked out his discards.

"What's your pleasure, mister . . . ?"

"John White. Two cards."

"They call me Rollo."

Dell fought back a chill, looking into those dark eyes for the first time, like hard slits in the light of the smoky candles of the wagon wheel chandelier overhead. Here was the coldblooded mastermind who'd struck his little county like a thunderbolt. A criminal larger, smarter, and more vicious than he'd ever arrested in his career — and one who had the wool over the eyes of everyone in El Paso as to the true nature of his business.

"Nice to meet'cha." Dell averted his gaze and picked up two fours, which made three of them in his hand. He raised fifty cents on the next round of bets.

"Nice to meet you. But I'm through with this hand." Rollo tossed his cards in the center. All the others folded with him, and Dell wished he'd only bet a quarter. Greenhorn move. He'd driven them out.

He took a deep breath and settled himself, focusing on the task at hand.

"You sure are winning tonight," another regular said after he'd won three more hands.

Dell merely nodded. "Night ain't over yet."

In the new hand, Dell had two aces to start with. Was this Rollo letting him win on purpose? No, no. The deal looked okay. Maybe it was just his lucky night. Oh Lord, how he hoped it was. If all hell broke loose later, he'd need every ounce of it to get out alive. All he could do was wait in the smoke-filled glare and see if his luck stayed with him. Two queens in the draw, and he held and lost the hand to a three of a kind.

The noise in saloon around them had grown steadily through the evening, with plenty of customers raising hell and dancing with the noisy whores working the place. It was like a factory. After a short courtship, the girls would whisk the anxious men back to their cribs before returning shortly for more business.

He glanced again at Rollo Magnus. The coldness of the man impressed him. He'd never had this much time to appraise an un-arrested criminal mind planted not five feet from him. Dell knew this man would kill him in the blink of an eye if he knew his real identity — a lawman that came a thousand horse miles to arrest him. That even made it sweeter.

But where was that death smell Angel had spoken about? *El olor de la muerte,* she'd called it. Maybe the cigar smoke and sour stink of the saloon and unwashed bodies in the place suppressed it. But he had less nose than most women had. He knew from his experiences with Connie and Guinn women could scent things that never entered his nostrils. He was close enough, now, to be sure. But no odor of death wafted across the table.

Guinn.

If he was shot down in this fiasco ahead, poor Guinn would need to find a new man. He'd left her far better off than Howard had, at least. It had knifed his heart leaving her — unwed, too. If he got out of there alive tonight and she got a divorce, he'd marry her in the shake of a lamb's tail. Damn, but he missed her.

His first wife had loved him and was loyal, but they never had the bond he had with Guinn. Connie had held back more. Had to be clothed all the time, awake or asleep. Any concession to being naked she shied from — even when they were alone. No one around, she wore something to hide her skin from the light or the dark. She told him several times when she dreamed of being left naked, it terrorized her. Even so, she'd been a lovely woman who cancer had stolen from him so fast — she'd been fine one day and dead the next. He'd grieved, and buried himself in his work as sheriff. Then he'd found Guinn . . . and something to really live for.

He had to survive tonight, had to bring this man and his outfit to justice. For the Thompsons and their children. For Rachel Combs.

And for him and Guinn.

By eleven-thirty, the crowd had thinned down some. Snyder came and got him out of the card game. He took him back through the curtained-off cribs, past the sounds of the world's oldest profession in full swing, and out the back door of the hotel. There across the alley stood a red-painted medicine wagon and two horses in harness.

They circled around to the back of the wagon, where a man Dell had never seen before waited. He greeted Snyder, then pulled the curtain aside to reveal five cowering, naked, brown-skinned young girls huddled inside.

In the dim light of a lantern, the unknown

man — was this Sanchez? — gave a sharp command in Spanish and the girls all stood up. Snyder took the candle lamp and held it up to show each individual girl to him. He made them turn around and walk a short distance. None were crippled, though they looked doped up and did as they were told obediently. Dell noticed marks on several of them from a quirt — probably the one the stranger carried on his wrist.

"We have a bed in here if you wish try any or all of them."

"Not here," Dell said. "Now, what if something happens and they don't get them to my place in Dallas?"

"Trust me. *Señor* Sanchez will deliver them. He does this all the time for us. And if something happens, we will send replacements."

"I know. I heard you were dependable. Here's the address to my place in Dallas. Don't deliver them in the damn daylight. Too many eyes around there." The address was in a residential area chosen by the Rangers.

"He won't do that."

"I pay you, and then you pay him?" Dell asked. "I'm just asking. Is that how it works?"

"Yes, all the money goes to me," Snyder

said. He turned to Sanchez, a snaky-looking man with greasy hair and acne-cratered skin. "Here is the address. No slip-ups."

"I know my business." He tossed a stack of simple gowns up to the slaves, telling them in Spanish to dress quickly. This done, Sanchez secured the cloth cover and moved toward the front of the wagon and the horses.

Dell reached into his vest and pulled out the money. The medicine wagon was already halfway down the alley as he started counting the bills into Snyder's hands.

Then, from out of the night came the words, *"Texas Rangers! Don't anyone move!"*

Dell slapped the last hundred-dollar bill into Snyder's palm, drew his .45, cocked it, and shoved it in his gut. "That means you, Slick."

"Who in the hell are you?"

"The man whose jail you unlocked back in my hometown a few weeks back." Dell growled, his finger itching on the trigger. "Now give me that money back and march yourself over to the doorway."

"You got him?" Curley Thomas asked from the doorway. "We got four of 'em out here."

"I got him. Anyone get Rollo?"

"No. Wait, he was he *here*?"

"He was earlier." *Damn it!* That son of a bitch had gotten away. "What about the girls and the wagon?"

"Cap'n Brooks and three more Rangers are stationed down on the border to pick them up as soon as they cross back into Texas."

"Good deal." He prodded Snyder in the back with his gun barrel. "Don't you make one false move, partner."

Thomas tossed him a pair of handcuffs. Stuffing the stack of money back in his vest pocket, Dell holstered his revolver and cuffed Snyder's hands behind his back. None too nicely, either.

"You're really the damn sheriff from up there?" the hotel owner asked in disbelief. He winced in pain as Dell cinched the cuffs tight.

"Yep. I came a long ways to get you bastards. You should be asking me what that Cody boy asked you when you unlocked his cell — what took you so long to get here?"

The Rangers all laughed at that.

Dell sat Snyder down with his compatriots and let one of the other Rangers slap him in leg irons. There they were, four of the men who'd committed such a heinous crime back home, all sitting in a line in a dusty alleyway, shackled hand and foot.

Thomas pointed them out.

"This one's Paulus," he said, nudging a dirty, rail-thin Mexican man with black eyes and a patchy beard. "He came late to the party. The short one here is Monte Garcia, and the big guy is Hidalgo Andre. And of course, you already know thine host, Philip Snyder."

"Don't count all your chickens till they're hatched," called a new voice from down the alley.

They looked up to see Captain Brooks riding up. Behind him were the medicine wagon, two more Rangers on horseback, and the teamster, Sanchez, trussed up and thrown belly-down over another mount. A third Ranger had taken his place driving the wagon.

"Looks like a clean sweep," Brooks said with a grin.

"Almost," Dell agreed. "But not quite. Magnus was here earlier, but we missed him. I don't know if he knows what's happened yet, but if he does. . . ."

"He'll be heading out of town in a big damn hurry," Thomas finished his sentence. The young Ranger looked up at his superior, still in the saddle. "Sir?"

Brooks didn't hesitate. "Go. Go get that sumbitch and bring him in. We've got all the evidence we need now."

Thomas raised an eyebrow. "Dell?"

"I'm damn sure willing. I just want this bunch secured until we can get him."

"We've got a wagon coming to take them to the best jail in the region," Brooks assured him.

"Then what the hell are we waiting for?"

Thomas pulled Sanchez off the horse and shoved him down in the dust with the others. Grabbing the reins, he tossed them to Dell. "Crocker, Dell's borrowing your horse. We'll have it back to you in the morning."

"It's yours, Curley."

"Let's ride." Thomas ran for his own mount as Dell swung into the saddle.

Brooks sidled his horse up beside him. "Dell, you ever need one damn thing, you call on us out here. We'll ride day or night to come help you. This is our slickest arrest, and a long time coming. There's no telling the women they have enslaved."

"Thank you, Cap'n. I sure do appreciate everything you and your boys have done."

Brooks punched him in the arm. "No problem. Now go get that bastard, he's all we lack. Good luck, Sheriff."

Thomas kicked his horse into motion.

"Wire El Paso for them to cover his house

and business — I bet he's running home to escape," he shouted as he shot by.

Dell spurred the fresh horse and rushed to catch up. Even with their success at rounding up the others, they'd only won half a victory so far tonight, and he knew it. They'd need a lot of luck to have any hope of catching up to him.

But, while Rollo Magnus was a slippery devil, at least his true colors had been finally been exposed. He could no longer live under the mantle of being a law-abiding citizen. No doubt his wealth would be taken away, and even should he escape, he'd be on the run for good. Or his head rolled out of a burlap sack to back a claim for the rewards piled on him — dead or alive. There was some comfort in that knowledge.

NINE

On jaded lathered horses at dawn, they met the El Paso Police guarding Magnus's locked storefront. "Ranger, what's going on here?" the sergeant demanded.

"We've been riding half the night to get here," Thomas told him. "Last night we busted up a slave sale down in Mesilla. Got the whole damn gang, except the ringleader."

"You can't mean Rollo Magnus?" the officer asked in disbelief.

"The same," the young Ranger said. "We've got all the evidence we need linking him to the slavers, and a barrel of other crimes, but he got away before we could make the arrest."

"That sumbitch and his gang murdered a family in my town," Dell added. "Last night they sold five teenage slaves to me as an undercover agent. They might be your own daughters. He's not a businessman like you all thought. He's a murdering rapist, thief, and slave dealer."

"How long have you had the storefront secured?" Thomas asked.

"Since just after two in the morning. Cap'n got a telegram from Mesilla."

"Nobody in or out?" Dell asked.

"No one, sir."

"And you've got the back covered, too?"

"Aye, that we do."

He looked at Thomas. "Try his house?"

"We have people standing guard there, as well," the policeman offered.

Thomas sat straight up in the saddle. "I know where it is. The horses had a break. Let's go."

They trotted the tired mounts to Magnus's house, where they found three more policemen and had to retell the very same story. Once they were convinced, Dell and Thomas turned their attention to Rollo's wife, an attractive young Hispanic woman named Isabella with a baby.

"He never came home," she cried, shedding great big tears. "I don't know where he's gone. I so worried."

While they were questioning the wife, two lawyers arrived at the house and demanded the police leave immediately. Their client, they said, had broken no laws and no one was guilty until proven so by a jury.

Dell waded into the middle of them. "That bastard's been living under that cover for too long. Last night, his men were caught by the Rangers with live slaves in their possession and money changing hands. *That* will stand up in any court, and it's just the beginning. Your client robbed a bank, murdered a family, raped the women, broke convicted felons out of jail, *and* gave them aid and comfort."

"And who are you?"

"Sheriff of Saddler County Texas. Where the crimes I just mentioned occurred."

The smaller one puffed out his chest. "You have no authority here."

"I do have some authority. I'm also a deputy US Marshal investigating a slavery ring, and your client is a prime suspect. Now we are going to search the house for evidence. Go back to your office. This is a federal task force investigation operation."

"I am contacting a federal official to have you jailed."

Dell rolled his eyes. "Curley, handcuff these two on the charges of obstructing justice in my investigation of the crime scene."

"So done, Marshal Hoffman."

Leaving the pair of lawyers in the hands

of the police outside, he and Thomas made a thorough search of the house. In the library, they found three letters from Ira Cody discussing details of the jailbreak and bank robbery — clear evidence implicating Magnus and his outfit in the crimes, as well as the murders committed during their commission. It would hang them all in the end, including Old Ira himself.

Curley Thomas initialed the pages, along with the date and location they'd been found, as corroboration of the evidence.

The lawyers were still hollering outside. Inside, the baby had stopped crying, but the mother nursing it hadn't.

"This locks up your case pretty tight, Dell," Thomas said.

"Yes, it does," he agreed. "But justice won't be done until we bring Magnus in."

"We'll get him. He can't run forever." The younger man sighed. "What do you want me to do with these damn lawyers?"

"Can't shoot 'em, can we?"

They laughed. Finally, Thomas went and unlocked them and sent them on their way. By that time, though, another problem had arisen. As they walked out of the garden gate into the street, they were swarmed with newspaper people demanding information.

Thomas held up his hands. "I am Ranger

Christopher Thomas. At four p.m. today, Texas Ranger Captain Harold Brooks and US Deputy Marshal Dell Hoffman will tell you all about this case down at Ranger Headquarters."

That seemed to satisfy the frenzy. The young Ranger, though, still seemed unsure.

He turned to Dell. "That sound okay to you?"

"Yeah, it did. 'Cept for one thing."

Thomas looked confused. "What's that?"

"I ain't never talked to no big-city press people before."

The news meeting actually started closer to five p.m., mostly because Dell was late. On the way back to Ranger Headquarters, he'd stopped by the Telegraph Office to cable the big news to his most important follower.

Guinn,
    Successfully captured all but Robert, the Cody boys, and Rollo. Have them all in jail here in El Paso. Lots more to tell. Look for me in two weeks.

                                    Love,
                                    Dell

Now, facing the gathered reporters, Captain Brooks held his hands up for quiet.

"Take your seats now, please.

"Hello to you all. The Texas Rangers have been very busy these past days, and we'd like to share some details about it all with you today.

"Dell Hoffman, a great lawman, a deputy US Marshal, and sheriff of Saddler County, came out here on horseback last week, alone and with no public funds. His mission — to apprehend a group of outlaws he'd tracked from Saddler County to El Paso. A group of outlaws that had robbed a bank, shot the bank president, and raped and murdered four members of that man's family — three of them children — all while in commission of another crime, opening the local jail up to aid the escape of two guilty murderers sentenced to hang.

"But more than that, he came with evidence to expose an El Paso businessman, a highly respected member of our community, not only as the ringleader of this gang he'd pursued, but as a slave trader, as well. And, my friends, that's exactly what he did, and in grand fashion.

"Assisting my department in our own investigation of this local slavery ring, Sheriff Hoffman went undercover across the state line to Mesilla, New Mexico, posing as a potential buyer of young Mexican girls to

169

work in a house of ill repute in Dallas. He made contact with the suspects in question and set up a deal to purchase five teenage Mexican girls for four hundred dollars apiece. When the deal was transacted, my Rangers were on the scene, and took four suspects into custody. We also arrested the operator of a medicine wagon contracted to deliver the slaves to Dallas as he crossed over into Texas — with the five females in his van, making it federal case. While the ringleader managed to escape, and is currently at large, make no mistake, this is a great victory for law enforcement. His criminal enterprises have been shut down, and his gang put in jail.

"Now, I'm proud to introduce my good friend, and the friend of all the citizens of El Paso, north and south, Sheriff Dell Hoffman."

Dell couldn't help but blush a little at such a flowery introduction. "Thank you, Captain. I'm much obliged to you and your Rangers for all you've done. I've never worked with a better group of lawmen in my life, and that's the truth.

"Folks, this bunch we arrested last night came to Saddler County about six weeks ago. The family of two men found guilty of murder paid them to break their grandsons out of jail. That family paid them several thousand dollars for those services, but it wasn't enough. They demanded more, so the family, in desperation, set them up to rob the local bank at the same time they broke the boys out. And that's exactly what they did.

"But they didn't just rob the bank. Oh, no. These animals took the banker's family hostage first and used them as leverage to force him to open the vault. Once he'd done that, they shot and killed him as a diversion to draw me, my deputy, and the town marshal away from the jail. As for the banker's family, they were of no more use — so they raped and murdered his wife, daughter, and two youngs sons to prevent there from being any witnesses to identify them."

There were gasps among the crowd of reports, a murmur of shock and disgust. Dell's own stomach turned at the memory of discovering the Thompson family that night, and for a moment, he could smell the coppery scent of blood on the air again. Thrusting his hands into the pockets of his britches, he cleared his throat and continued.

"With the money in hand and local law distracted, the gang finally did what they'd been hired to do. They walked into my jail and let those two boys loose. Gave them money and horses to escape. But they were smart. They didn't just release those two prisoners. They opened every cell and let 'em all out — more than thirty of 'em — so me and my deputies would have a harder time running them all down figuring out what really happened.

"Folks, this was the most brutal, cold-blooded, and carefully-planned crime I've ever seen or heard of in my time as a lawman. Five murders. Two rapes. A bank robbed. A mass jailbreak. With hardly any evidence and no living witnesses, I had to start at the bottom, put things together piece by piece. But when I finally found a name and description, it was of a man nobody believed could have done it — Rollo Magnus.

"I sent a telegram about the man to Captain Brooks here in El Paso. He sent back to tell me I was barking up the wrong tree, that Magnus was a respected business-man here and couldn't have been all the way up in Saddler. But my gut told me the evidence I had was right. So I left my bride-to-be, saddled up my horse, and came on down here myself. With the help of the Rangers, I went undercover and set up this

172

deal to buy slave girls for a whorehouse, and then, just as it was about to happen, guess who showed up, right there in Mesilla at the hotel I was at? That's right. Rollo Magnus. Turns out breaking felons out of jail, robbing banks, and raping and murdering women and children are only a small part of the criminal enterprise he ran, right here in El Paso. But let me tell you, now his goose is cooked. We didn't get him last night, but some bounty hunter out there will one day. They'll shoot him, chop off his head with an axe, and bring it back in a gunny sack for the reward, save Texas the cost of the hanging bill."

Brooks clapped him on the back. "Amen."

"And that's all I've got."

The reporters had plenty of questions, but Dell was done in. Leaving Brooks to deal with them, he left the stage. He'd done what he'd came here to do. It was time to go home.

He found Curley Thomas filling out reports in an empty office and said his goodbyes. Next he went to retrieve his horses out from Juanita, the sweet Mexican lady who'd kept them for him. She was so pleased to hear he'd saved those girls the night before, she refused to accept his money. Hugging him fiercely, she kissed his cheeks and thanked him for his work. Then she helped him saddle the horses, and replenished his food supplies from her own pantry.

Heading out of town, he passed Ranger Headquarters one last time and saw Brooks still out on the front steps, talking to the press, now with Thomas at his side. The Rangers stopped when they saw Dell, and raised their hands in salute. Whew. There were some real lawman.

Dell smiled, tipped his hat, and rode away.

It took a day and half to make Big Springs. He bought some more supplies there and then rode on, numb and dumb in the saddle for two weeks until he crossed the high place and knew he was within a day of home.

Finally, he rode all night in a soft, unusual rain. Midsummer rains usually died within an hour or so after sundown, but this one refused. If he hadn't known the way so well, he'd have been forced to stop and find shelter. But the thought of Guinn kept him going, and he pushed Burt and the pack-horse on because he couldn't stop short of home. Of her.

The sun was trying to wake up the rain-soaked world by the time he finally reined up outside the house. He was in the alleyway behind the barn, trying to loosen wet latigoes to unload his saddle and pack-saddle, when he heard a sigh behind him.

"Dell Hoffman, you stubborn old cow-puncher. You used to come upstairs and get me to help you do that."

Dell turned and came face-to-face with the thing that had been on his mind day and night since the moment he'd left for El Paso. Guinn stood before him in the watery light of dawn, dressed in nothing but a thin nightgown, her hands on her hips. She was beautiful, radiant, determined. Without a thought, he scooped her up into his arms and held her tightly to him.

"Lord God, am I happy to see you, Guinn."

"What are you doing out here?"

"I wanted to be unloaded, had a bath, and shaved before you found me home. I rode all damn night in this blessed rain that never stopped." He held her by her shoulders and felt ready to cave in. "I've missed you so much, but I got to get these two unsaddled. They've been through hell for me, God love 'em."

"Sit on that trunk." She moved him force-fully to a nearby seat and made him sit. Then she turned back to the horses. He watched as she undid the double girth, took

175

the packsaddle and pads off Rod, and set them aside. The horse wandered off to get a drink, and Dell started to get up. "I can do this."

She held up a hand. "Save yourself. I've got Burt."

"Guinn, I came home soon as I could. I got 'em. Well, most of 'em. The ones who did it. But Rollo got away."

"I know you haven't seen a newspaper." She grunted and finally got the wet latigo loose, and Burt's saddle slipped off. She let it fall in the hay and dust, then she jerked the saddle pads off. Next she pulled the bit from his mouth, and the gelding staggered off with his partner for a drink.

Guinn swept up her nightgown tail out of the littered floor. "You ever hear of making love in the hay?"

He managed a tired smile. "That was only for kids, I thought."

She jerked her head toward the back corner of the barn. "That hay stack looks plumb inviting. How hard is your bedroll to get loose?"

"I —" he started to get up.

She stopped him. "I can get it. Stay there."

Guinn went to the saddle and pried the rawhide strings loose. The bedroll rolled out like a tongue on her and she laughed. She bent over, rolled it up again, took it up in the deeper hay, and spread it out.

"It isn't level but who cares."

She came back to him, kneeled, and twisted off his boots. Her laughter rolled over him like the wings of an angel. "Take off your clothes. That is all I can do for you."

Dell shook his head, his fingers fumbling with buttons and wet fabric. To encourage him, she stood up and shed her long gown, pulling it over her head. It was something Connie would never have done, a side of herself she never showed him. Leave it to Guinn.

He was home.

TEN

Dell woke up to a sneezing fit. When he'd finished, he turned his watering eyes to the bed beside him and met Guinn's knowing gaze. They laughed.

"How long have I slept?"

"Not for a full twenty-four hours yet, but close to it," she said. "You must be famished. I brought you some food on a tray."

He scrubbed at his whiskered face. "I'm dirty as an old dog, got more whiskers than a billygoat, and stink like a wagon run over a skunk, and here you are wearing a bathrobe in a hay pile. Lord girl, you tempt me."

Guinn put the tray of food in his lap and handed him a folded piece of paper. "Eat and read."

Dear Sheriff Hoffman,

The request for Mrs. Howard's divorce has been handled and processed by my court, and the papers with the completed divorce decree will be posted forthwith from Austin to Mrs. Howard at her home address. Her divorce is final.

Sincerely,
Judge Charles Ransom

"Holy cow! This means we can get married."

"When?"

"Before I left home, my momma told me one thing I must always remember — If I ask a woman to marry me, let her set the date. Period."

"You figured that out?"

"Figured what out?"

"Why she said it that way."

Dell scratched his head. "I'm not sure I understand what you're getting at."

She laughed. "For such a big, tough lawman, you can be incredibly dense, my love. It has to do with the curse of Eve. Why do you think she said 'period' at the end?"

"Oh. I —" He stopped, flustered. It really did make more sense now. "You got that?"

She shook her head.

"How come?"

Guinn gave him the biggest smile he'd ever seen. "Because I may be —"

"And I rode off and left you?" He stared at her in cold disbelief, his mouth gaping.

With a small giggle, she shrugged. "I missed one. I'm twenty-eight and it's never happened before."

"My first wife missed some, but the babies never lived."

"I'm just saying the date doesn't matter because of anything to do with that." She looked up into the sky. "God willing, this one will survive."

Dell set the tray aside. He'd had enough breakfast, or supper, or whatever damn meal this was supposed to be. Pulling her to him, he parted her robe and kissed her.

A few days later, the town had a barbecue in his honor at the Methodist Church, and, in a first for the town, even the Baptists came to celebrate his return. Billy Lee — who also served as mayor in addition to Justice of the Peace — presented Dell with an engraved gold pocket watch on behalf of all the grateful citizens of the county. Then, in a ceremony witnessed by the entire town, he united Dell and Guinn in the bonds of holy matrimony.

They were cheered and toasted by the whole county. Guinn wore a pretty, lacey white dress that she and Nan had sewn up, while Dell wore a suit and a new Boss of the Plains Stetson hat a couple of local ranchers had bought for him. Henry Harrison, owner of the big HBH ranch outside of town, offered them the use of a secluded cabin on his spread for their honeymoon.

After several more hours of celebration, they boarded a buckboard loaded with supplies and headed out of town. The matched buckskin team pulling them belonged to another Saddler County rancher — Clark Day — and was borrowed special to deliver the newlyweds out to the HBH and their honeymoon destination.

"You were sure quiet saying 'I do' today."

Dell glanced over at his new bride and laughed. Guinn had one hand on his shoulder and the other wrapped around the edge of the springseat as he slid them through another corner. Her hat had slid back on her head and was threatening to blow off completely. "Do I need to slow down?"

"I can handle it if you can, cowboy." She smiled. "Now what were you saying? About earlier?"

"I was just so damned choked up. Couldn't find how to get my voice back." He shook his head. "I rode out of here near a month ago thinking I'd spend the rest of my ornery life looking for them turkey buzzards that broke the serenity of Saddler County. I figured I'd never have you for my wife, or that we'd ever have kids or anything.

Then I came home to you worn half-dead, and there you were unsaddling my horses in a nightgown and rolling in the haystack with me. How could I find my voice when you finally really were mine? No more sneaking around. No more hiding our lovemaking. You should have been there the night I sweated out buying them little girls, just before we arrested that bunch. Why, they were little brown schoolgirls, all of them naked and obedient. Snyder asked me if I wanted to sample them. It made me sick, but I had to act like nothing was wrong and keep going. I was giving Snyder the money when I heard Curley Thomas shout, " 'Texas Rangers! Put your hands up.' " I stuck my gun in that damn Snyder's guts and would have shot him, but all I could think about was you, and those scared, naked little girls. That's why I got so choked up when it came time to say 'I do.' "

They slid around the next corner, and Guinn reached up and kissed the fire out of him.

It grew dark as they bumped over the last few miles, and he had to depend on the team tracing their way through the twilight between the live oak and cedars. He finally spotted the cabin in the starlight, and told her they were there. He brought the team

182

to a halt, then reached back into the buckboard and found the lamp he'd brought along with them. Striking a match, he lit it, and led her up the steps. At the door, he set down the light and carried her over the threshold.

Guinn gasped. The cabin was no simple settler's place, but a four-bedroom palace with a huge dining room, living room, and kitchen. The Harrisons had built it a few years back for family reunions and such, and stocked it with comfortable furniture and a collection of stuffed Texas game animals. They lit several more lamps and explored it together, moving from room to room and gaping at the luxury. They ended up in the kitchen, where Guinn set about making supper on the stove while Dell sat and drank a steaming cup of coffee.

"You hear that big owl hoot when we pulled up?" he asked.

"I sure did," she replied. "And listen to those coyotes."

"Texas music."

She hugged him. "I bet you heard lots of things riding out there and back by yourself."

"It wasn't no Sunday picnic, but it was worth it. I'm just glad I went and got that crew arrested. They didn't believe Magnus was selling slaves when I got to El Paso. They couldn't believe he'd done the deal back here. No one could catch him and his buddies."

"My Texas sheriff did."

"Oh, Guinn, it ain't over." Dell sighed. "Them Cody boys are still out loose, and that man Rollo is still at large. I'd hoped the case in El Paso would bring enough attention for the rest of 'em to be brought in, but we haven't heard a thing since I got back."

She put a heaping plate on the table in front of him. "Put it out of your mind for now and eat your first supper as my husband."

"Yes ma'am. And you looked beautiful in that wonderful white dress."

"You are far too easy to please, Delbert."

"Hey. That's only for legal usage."

"I won't speak of it again," she said it with a sly little grin. "I really love this place."

"Much as I love it for our purpose, it does beat the barn."

Days passed, but for Dell and his bride there existed nothing but the simple joys found in one another and the future that awaited them together. They rode endlessly across the lands of the HGH ranch on their borrowed horses, laughing, teasing, drinking in the beauty of the Texas summer, making love whenever and wherever the mood would strike. It was a week of heavenly union, and it was over far too quickly for their liking.

As they drove the buckboard home the following Saturday, Dell asked her if being pregnant made her feel any different.

"Not really," she said. "I have indigestion some mornings. I keep expecting morning sickness, but nothing's come up yet. Not that I'm complaining. I am sure pleased I haven't had any different reaction to it."

"Me, too."

"I'm worried some about our horseback riding, though," she continued, "and I probably won't ride anymore. Doc Kelton said riding in later pregnancy might not be the best thing to do. But he also said he thinks I'm healthy enough to carry to full term. He can't tell me why Howard and I didn't have children. But in a way, I'm grateful for that. Our marriage ended so badly. . . ."

He nodded. "I understand."

"I was little shocked about it the week after you left and I had no period. I didn't want to write you and worry you way out there, and I was fine." Guinn brushed a lock of hair out of her face and tucked it behind her ear. "Now two months have gone by without one, and I can't say I feel it."

Dell reached over and squeezed her knee under her denim skirt. "I'm proud we're on this road together. It'll complete our marriage to have kids. You're smart and educated and our children will be, too. We live in a very changing time. Steam engines, telegraphs. . . . Hell, little things like barbed wire are changing everything. It'll change land ownership. It's already closing the cattle trails. Railroads soon will be everywhere. If we can ever get over the debt from the war and do something about these crazy up-and-down money cycles that paralyze progress, we may become a great country."

Guinn laughed.

"What's so funny?"

"You," she said. "We live in this little Texas cowtown, and you get worked up about these big things that seem so far away."

"They may seem far away, but they're not really. We'll be feeling them here soon."

"I know you worry about those things, but canning summer vegetables and homegrown meat is big business and makes people self-sufficient. Nan and I have filled two cellars with garden food this year. And it's all safe to eat if you boil it."

"I still like good smoked jerky, but I know it's a chore to preserve it."

"Nan's watching my hens while we've been gone, and I bought two shoats to fatten at her house. You'll see what we can do."

"You're a dream girl." Dell sighed happily. "I'm not the smartest man in this world, but I appreciate you and your ways. All of them. I am not being critical of Connie — God rest her soul — but she always had to be wearing something. I mean foot to neck. It doesn't bother you to fool around with me in private and not have any clothes on. I just love that you trust me like that. If that poor girl even dreamed she got caught nude, it upset her."

Guinn waved it away. "That's just me. I feel so safe with you, I don't need clothes unless it embarrasses you."

"Don't change. I love it that way."

"Good. I don't recall doing that much until you and I began our affair. Howard always was worried someone would see me. You sure love me more than he ever did. I like that." She snuggled against him on the spring seat. "To me, my man's attention shouldn't be worship, but it should be intimate. It makes me feel like I have a space of my own in your life. I know you appreciate me. You know it goes the other way, too."

"There wasn't a day went by out there I didn't think about you," he said. "Don't ever be concerned about me and other women — they don't spark any interest in me whatsoever."

"Dell Hoffman, we've found a suitable life. Don't change it or be one ounce different. And while I may get big as a bear, don't stop loving on me. You won't hurt the baby." She reached up and kissed him.

"Let's stop in town get the mail. You need anything from the store?"

"No, but you can stop and check on Wilbur. He's done well as your replacement, but he's glad you're back." She grinned. "While you were gone, he reminded me of a tomcat in a room full of rockers. Afraid he'd get his tail smashed."

"Thanks, sweetheart."

Wilbur was excited to see them when they stopped by the jail. They chatted about the wedding and caught up on the local gossip for a while, but soon things turned to business.

"Ain't no news on them damn Cody brothers," Wilbur said with a shake of his head. "I won't forget that bathtub thing if I ever need information out of a hardcase again. I thought we'd drown Ira before he gave anything up and we'd never know who was here."

"Ira came in without a fuss — remember

that." Dell leaned against his desk and took off his hat. "He just needed a little encouragement. His son chose to die when you went for him."

"Yeah, but it was sure tough."

"We needed information and it wasn't coming fast enough."

"Were they like you thought they'd be?" Wilbur asked. "The outlaws, I mean. What were they like?"

"I played cards with Rollo," Dell told him. "I didn't smell no death on him like Angel did, but he's sure cold-blooded to look at. Gave me chills. Cold, calculating, self-centered. I think he came out to Mesilla to look me over, like he had psychic powers to tell if I was real or not."

"Were those women you bought purty?"

"Hell, Wilbur, they were just little girls. Sad thing to see. They looked pitiful and scared. They'd been beaten and doped up, too. Snyder thought I might use 'em to see how they were. Even offered me a test bed."

"What did you do?"

He snorted. "Told him I was confident he'd given me good girls and hoped like hell the Rangers would show up soon."

"Were you scared?"

"I was sitting on pins and needles. There were four of those *hombres* lined up behind

189

me. One wrong move. . . ." Dell traced a finger across his neck. "Thank the Lord Curley Thomas arrived when he did and rounded them up. Then Brooks arrested the medicine wagon man as he drove over the Texas border. Made it a federal crime. Some lawyers said the other arrests were illegal because we'd done it in New Mexico, but I had my US Deputy Marshal badge and told them the Rangers had been deputized to assist me. Hell, they'd brought those girls up through Texas on the way to New Mexico, already."

"What did they do with the girls?"

"Gave 'em to some Catholic sisters. If they'd been kidnapped, they were to be returned to their families. The others — the ones who were sold into it by their parents — are up for adoption by people who will care for them."

Wilbur shook his head again. "Does that kind of thing really still happen?"

"I think so. Rumor has it in Mexico a blonde girl in that age group can bring a couple thousand dollars. They thought about doing that to the Thompson girl, Judy. Rollo told them they couldn't conceal her good enough to carry her that far." He shrugged. "That medicine wagon deal's what got me. How many of those things have come right through here while I've been sheriff? How many girls could we have saved if we'd looked in one? How many have been taken right under our nose? Like that Branch girl a couple years back?"

"Hard to say," Wilbur said, looking down at the floor.

"Hard to understand," Dell agreed.

They were silent for a moment, thinking the whole thing over. Then Wilbur snapped his fingers. "Almost forgot. That Emerson Bunch and Circle H are really butting heads up north of here. Couple of hands from the Circle H got into it with the two oldest Emerson boys, Cy and Walt. No one got the best of it. Doc ended up stitching on the four of them. Cy broke his arm. One of the cowboys lost part of his ear, and they all four had black eyes and bruises. I couldn't tell who started it, but I told them to quit fighting or I'd lock them all up next time. That wasn't a friendly fist fight. That was attempted manslaughter."

He sighed. No rest for the weary. "I'll get settled in, ride up there one day this next week and see if I can sort the troublemakers out."

"Good. For my money, that war ain't over."

"Any more problems?"

191

The deputy opened up a ledger on the desk and leafed through a couple of pages. "I jailed couple guys for drunk and disorderly. That Hamby boy's wife, Artie, run off with some cowboy from the Pearl Ranch. Rudy came busting in here saying she'd been kidnapped. I rode clear to Sach Water, found them living in a deserted cabin, happy as two peas in a pod. She told me she had all that wimpy ex-husband she could stand and found her a real man. Well — that's cleaning up her version so I could tell it to folks."

Dell laughed. "She's Jim Boyles's daughter?"

"That's the one. And she's always been wild, ain't she?"

"Mustang wild. Hamby wasn't tough enough to marry her."

"She'd run off on me, I'd clap my hands." The deputy closed the ledger. Wilbur had always been steady, but he seemed to have grown up a lot in the last few months. Well, hadn't they all? "Hey, once you get settled back in, I want to take my wife to see her sister down at Junction. Her sister ain't been well and she wants to see if she can help her out."

"When would you like to go?"

"You all right here week after next?"

Dell nodded. "Go. You ain't had any time off in two months. What's wrong with her?"

"Alice ain't sure."

"Handle it. And tell Alice thanks for all the work she did on our wedding. Guinn and I sure appreciated it."

"You two make a great couple. You were lucky to find her, she's some lady. Always thought that ex-husband of hers needed his head examined leaving her like that."

"I knew you did, but we were slipping around keeping a secret going. I couldn't say a thing to back you up." He smiled. "Let her tell folks, but so you know, we're going to have a baby soon, if the good Lord's willing."

"Lucky you!"

"Thanks, partner."

Things seemed like they were — blessedly — back to normal in the county. And yet, happy as he was, Dell still felt uneasy. Something still gnawed at his gut.

Guinn had kept all the newspaper stories related to his El Paso excursion, and the capture of the slavers was big news across the state and beyond. Lawmen all over the land had been made aware of the human trafficking ring, and were checking every medicine wagon that showed up in their counties and towns. Snyder, Sanchez, and the other three *pistoleros* were awaiting trial and, God willing, would never taste free air again.

It was bittersweet, though. Dell Hoffman was no fool. Yeah, so maybe he'd curbed some of it. But if those clowns were in jail, someone else was already filling the void, finding some other way to sell and transport young female slaves across the border. He'd never forget the image of those young girls standing in the back of that wagon, naked and trembling. It was a scene as tragic to him as the bloody bodies he'd found in the Thompson house that night.

And the man responsible for it all was still out there somewhere.

Rollo Magnus.

Dell sighed and put his hat back on his head. He strode out of the jail and down the steps, heading for the waiting buckboard with his new wife on the seat.

Guinn turned to him and smiled, then froze, her green eyes wide.

"Dell —"

"Hold it right there, you sumbitch."

His heart stopped.

Who in the hell was that?

The town and boardwalks were full of people out on Saturday morning. From somewhere behind him, a women screamed.

His own wife shouted, "Watch out, Dell. He's got a gun."

Dell listened to the uneven thump of boots on wood coming closer from off to his right. Whoever it was, they were on the boardwalk in front of the saddle shop next door to the jail.

"What do you want?" he asked without turning around.

"What you think I want, you no-good shit," came the slurred reply. "Turn around!"

Slowly, hands raised at his sides, Dell turned to face his assailant. Hatless and haggard, Buster Combs stood on the saddle shop steps twenty feet away, his dirty gray hair hanging in his face. He looked drunk and used up, the gun in his hand pointed unsteadily at Dell's chest. At this range, it was moving too much to be at all accurate, but with so many people on the street, if he fired, someone was bound to get hit.

"Buster —"

"You killed my wife," Buster yelled, cutting him off. "You killed Rachel! So now . . . Now I'm gonna kill yers, right before I kill you."

The old man cocked the hammer and Dell's hand dropped to his holster. Before his own barrel could clear the leather, a shotgun blast tore Buster near in half and dropped him facedown into the dust of the street.

Dell spun, revolver drawn and finger on the trigger.

Harry Connor, the town's string-bean master carpenter, stood white-faced on his porch with a smoking Greener in his hands, surrounded by a cluster of sunbonnets all close to fainting with their hands clenched over their ears or mouths.

"All right, Harry?"

Shaking like a leaf, Connor lowered the shotgun and shook his head like a man that's taken a blow to the head. "All — all right, Dell."

Feeling his own hand shaking from the adrenaline in his bloodstream, Dell holstered his .45 and walked slowly over to Buster's lifeless form. The pistol lay in the dirt beside him, cocked and ready to fire, shining dully in the late morning light. Buster had never had the chance to pull the trigger.

He picked up the revolver and lowered the hammer. "Rest easy, Buster. I never did that to your wife."

"Dell!" Guinn slammed into him, tears streaming down her pretty face. He held her close, rocking her from side to side and giving silent thanks that she hadn't been harmed. Behind her, Wilbur burst through the jail door, shotgun in hand. His jaw dropped as he took in the scene around them.

"You okay, Dell?"

"I'm fine. Buster's the only one who ain't." He jerked his head toward the carpenter, still standing stock-still on the porch across the street. "Harry took him down before he could pull the trigger."

"Thank God for Harry."

Damn straight, Dell thought. Damn straight.

After a minute, Guinn settled down a bit, and he was able to take her by the hand and lead her away from the body. He mounted the steps to the carpentry shop, and squeezed Harry Connor's shoulder in gratitude.

"Harry," he said softly.

Connor looked at him with watery eyes, but nodded courteously. "Dell."

"I know that was the toughest thing you ever had to do in your life. But for all the people here today who could have been shot or killed, you have my thanks."

"It was hard. But when I was twelve and home alone, my best stock dog came home acting strange. Slobbering, growling. I knew he had rabies, just like Combs there had it today." Connor took a deep breath, wiped his face with his shirtsleeve. "It was much harder for me at that age to shoot him than this was."

Slowly, Dell reached down and eased the shotgun out of Connor's shaking grasp, then handed it to another man. "I want you to know that you did the right thing. I know how religious you are, and this must burn your heart. But God must have known you were the only one could stop him from killing us. He knows people can be cruel and must be stopped. Today you did it for the safety of all these people in town."

The carpenter nodded numbly. "Thanks, Dell. I can make peace now with him and my heart."

Crisis over, the crowd started to thin out a bit. Wilbur came over to find him, told him he'd take care of the body and meet with Billy Lee and Doc. In the meantime, Dell and Guinn should head home, and he'd stop by later to get an official statement.

"You're a good man, Wilbur."

His deputy laughed. "Nothing good about it. I just want you back in this office instead of me."

On the short ride home, Guinn was quiet.

Too quiet.

"Still got the shakes?" he asked gently.

"No. Just thanking the good Lord for keeping us safe this morning. That man was —" She stopped, hesitated. "He wanted to kill us."

"He didn't know what he was doing. He was old and tired, filled with grief over what happened to Rachel."

"I'm damn lucky to have a man as strong as you are and so dedicated to his work."

"Just doing my job. That's all."

"No, Dell it's how you handle situations like that one."

"I still haven't caught those two murderers again. Or Rollo Magnus."

"Not yet. But you caught me, didn't you?" She put a hand on her belly. "And you helped make the world a little bigger and better, God willing."

He hugged her. "If not, we'll always have each other."

"Yes, but you'll have to stand a roly-poly wife before it gets here."

"I can't wait. We've waited a long time to do this."

"I'll keep my fingers crossed and pray."

"If it doesn't work, we can always try it again."

"Yes. That option is always available." They both laughed.

ELEVEN

Weeks passed with no word of Rollo Magnus or the Cody brothers. Dell came to believe that the earth had simply swallowed them up. He wrote personal letters to fellow lawmen from across the state asking them to keep watch. The Cody boys would probably stay in Mexico, and according to Hal Brooks, there was no sign at all of Magnus in the El Paso/Juarez area, but they were still looking hard.

In the meantime, life went on in Saddler County. Someone stole three horses from the Thomas ranch while the family was gone to town shopping. Wilbur took down the description of the three animals and their brands. There was no telling who may have been passing through, taken the horses, and gone on. They'd likely never be seen again. But it was the most serious crime in the county and almost the hardest to solve. The prize for that one came when someone stole a wheelbarrow from the Buckner farm south of town. When it was recovered half a day later on the Fort Worth Road, Wilbur made the remark that he'd never before heard of anyone in Texas stealing anything to work with. They had a good laugh to brighten their day.

The Texas State Auditors finally finished their accounting of the bank robbery and put the total loss in cash, coin, and property at over fifteen thousand dollars. While most of the bank loans were still sound, and a banker came from San Angelo every two weeks to make collections on debts due, the loss was a serious financial problem for the town and its businesses. The money from the loans would eventually pay about twenty-five cents on the dollar back to bank account holders, but it would require years for them to break even — and only then if the economy stayed steady. That was the rub, though. Things kept going up and down like a yo-yo on a string, so there were no guarantees. In Texas, there was only one sure way to make a buck — by taking cattle to Kansas. The folks who did used their newfound money to buy more land. They said a steer in Kansas's value could buy ten acres of Texas ranch land. That ten acres could run a cow and calf, and folks went up there with a herd soon had ranches. Unless you had money coming in from the cattle drives, you were pretty much out of luck. And in spite of the ranches scattered about, some more prosperous than others, Saddler County hadn't had a major cattle drive in years.

So the town and its people dealt with things as best they could. Some families moved away. A couple of businesses closed. The bank down the street stayed shuttered. No one was interested in opening a new one in a place that could be a ghost town in the next couple of years.

Dell watched it all with the same mounting sense of guilt that had eaten at him for months. The robbery and jailbreak had happened on his watch. The bastards had planned it all right under his nose, and he never even got a whiff that something was amiss. Some lawman he'd turned out to be. Now the people of the town were paying the price for his incompetence.

Then one day a couple of months after Buster's death, he got a letter from El Paso, from a Ranger he'd known a few years back.

Dell,
  I was in Mesilla last week and talked to a man who told me the Cody Broth-

ers were tired of Mexico and planning to drift north soon, maybe ending up in Nebraska or Montana. He said they never mentioned Texas except that they'd have to travel through it on their way north. Thought you'd like to know so you could spread the word and be on the lookout.

Hap Dunken

Dell sat down immediately and wrote Hap a thank-you note. Mexico wasn't a great place if you weren't proficient in Spanish and had ran out of money — probably why the Cody boys were on their way back. Now all that was left to do was run them down.

He'd write an all-points telegram to the Rangers and state's main law officials. Maybe they would pass the news on for him.

Next, he met with Ulysses Snow, the county postman, and asked the old man to watch the mail coming to and from every member of the Cody family still in Saddler County. They wouldn't be dumb enough to use their real name on the envelope, but an address from some far-off place might give him clues to their location, especially if more than one letter came. Though usually ornery as a mad raccoon, Snow agreed, and promised him daily reports.

Dell began checking around the "camps" where the county riffraff and unemployed cowboys hung out. On one such trip, he even visited Tilly and found her surprisingly cordial. When he declined her offer of services, she laughed. "A real cowboy gentleman. I think you're the first I seen in these parts."

He tipped his hat. "Your servant, ma'am."

Busy brushing her graying, shoulder-length hair, Tilly looked closely at him in the vanity mirror. "I heard Buster Combs came after you a while back. Were you about to go to see God?"

Dell snorted. "Drunk as he was, he'd probably have killed some innocent women or children before he ever got close to me. The town was crowded that day."

"I wondered why Rachel killed herself. You know why? Word is Buster blamed you."

"Rollo Magnus stayed at her house while they made the deal to bust the boys out of jail. Raped her every night."

"That all?" Tilly put the brush down. "If I thought that way, I'd have committed suicide a hundred times."

"Different lives. You're a survivor, Tilly. To Rachel, it was the worst thing that had ever happened to her. After she told me about it,

I guess she couldn't live with herself anymore."

"So that's why Buster blamed you?"

"Yep." He nodded. "She told me and not him."

She went back to brushing her hair. "So what brings you out here this time? After another one of my clients?"

"Nah. Same one. Hear tell the Cody boys might be on the move again, coming back this way from Mexico on their way up north. You heard from Otis at all?"

"Not a word. Nothing at all since he rode out of town."

"And you'd tell me if you did this time?"

"Dell, I don't want no more trouble." Tilly shook her head. " 'Sides, I think he done forgot me for some *puta* south of the border."

She laughed, and Dell couldn't help but join her. Tilly was comfortable and at ease. If her manner was anything to go by — and she'd never been a very good liar — he could be satisfied she hadn't heard from them.

That evening Guinn had a big time teasing him. "You weren't even tempted by her?"

"Lord, no." He rolled his eyes.

"The way your wife is swelling up, I

wouldn't be surprised if you did."

"That's crazy. I'm so pleased we are going to have a baby, I could bust my buttons about it."

"Oh, Dell, I know you are. I'm simply disappointed with my shape. Not you or the baby. Ten years ago I might have accepted it easier."

"You'll be yourself again." He put an arm around her. "Don't worry. I count you at the top of the list of my things I'm proud of. I want to find your ex and hug him for leaving you."

She laughed loudly. "I could buy that, too."

Later that week, Elbert Willows came to town with the lifeless body of his wife, Clare. She'd been brutally raped and murdered, and Willows was in tears when he arrived at the jail with her bloody body wrapped in a blanket. Dell took one look at the bundle in the wagon bed and sent for Doc and Billy Lee.

Then he turned his attention to the distraught farmer.

"Who'd have done this?" he asked.

"I have no idea." Willows sniffled and wiped at his wet cheeks. "I come home at sundown and found her on the floor. I must have cried all night. I ain't done nothing to nobody. Why did they kill my wife?"

"I don't know, Elbert. Did you find the murder weapon?"

The farmer peered at him. "I don't know. I haven't eaten. I haven't done anything."

"I'll go get him a tray of food while we wait on the others," Wilbur said.

"Be best," Dell agreed. He turned back to Willows. "Did they steal anything?"

"No. I checked that. It was still hid where we put it."

"What? What was hidden?"

Willows looked at him blankly. "Why, the money, Dell."

"What money?"

"Mine." He shook his head. "I never trust banks. Like this one went broke, huh?"

"Did you ever mention your money to anyone?"

"I don't think so, Sheriff. Maybe I said that — that I don't use banks since they're all crooks."

"Who might've heard that?" Dell pressed.

"Maybe some guys after the robbery?"

"Who was present at the time?"

"I can only recall a few faces. I was playing cards at the saloon here in town, drinking a few beers."

"You keep thinking about it. One of those

men may be responsible for your wife's death."

"Clare never hurt a soul. I was so proud of her. I was lucky to have her. She was so beautiful." Willows shook his head and cried some more.

"You and her ever fight?"

"Fight? No. Anyone can tell you I bragged about her all the time."

Dell considered this. The first suspect in a murder is always the husband. Could the girl have done something to upset him enough to kill her? Taken up with some cowboy at one of the local ranches? It wasn't unheard of, and there was a large age difference between them. Clare couldn't have been a day over fifteen when Willows married her, and he was at least as old as Dell. She wasn't from around here, either. She was a Chelsea — hill people from up in Arkansas or Tennessee. When they married, Willows took her away from everything and everyone she knew.

A knock on the door broke up Dell's train of thought. He looked up to find Doc at the door. "What d'ya say, Doc?"

The doctor tipped his hat. "Morning, Dell. I saw the body outside. Mister Willows, please accept my deepest sympathies for your loss."

"Th— thank you, sir."

"Dell, I'm having the body taken to the undertaker's so I can examine it. I'll have a report for you later this afternoon."

"Good." Dell hoisted himself up out of his chair and walked around his desk. "While you're doing that, I'll ride out to the Willows' place and look around."

"What about me?" Willows asked.

"You stay right here, Elbert. Wilbur's on his way with lunch, and Billy Lee will be along to take your statement any minute. I'll be back in a few hours and we'll talk more."

Leaving Willows in Doc's care, Dell walked outside, unhitched his horse, and rode off in the direction of his house. Guinn came out on the porch as he reined up, drying her hands on a green tea towel.

"What'cha up to, cowboy?"

He shook his head. "Someone murdered Elbert Willows's young wife last night. Clare. I'm going to ride over and look at the scene, see what I can make of things."

"But why kill her?" she asked.

"I think they wanted his money."

"He have very much?"

"I'm not certain, but she was a horrible bloody mess. Wanted to let you know I may be late for supper."

"No problem." She threw him a kiss and sent him on his way. The woman was his guiding light.

Dell reached the Willows ranch house about midafternoon, the stock dogs barking up a storm as he dismounted at the corral. He'd seen tracks in the dirt on the ride up, and didn't want to disturb the ground around the hitch rack.

Walking carefully, he surveyed the sandy loam in front of the hitching post. The boot prints in the dust were small, and the right one had a hole in it. These were not Elbert Willows's boots, nor were the freshly-shod hoof prints and horse apples from the horse that had been tied there for more than a few hours. So Clare *did* have a visitor — and he'd left behind a calling card.

The house itself was a mess. A chair with a rope coiled around the legs stood empty in the middle of the front room. Broken glass crackled everywhere under his feet, the shattered remains of broken dishes and lamps. A cracked flour bin lay on its side on the floor behind the dry sink, its contents spread all over the kitchen floor. Someone had tied the Willows girl up and then torn the place apart, looking for something. But for what? Willows' money? Or something else?

When he stepped into the bedroom, Dell stopped short. The red-stained sheets had been torn from the bed, clothes were scattered around like trash, and the rankling odors of blood, excrement, and fear hung heavy in the air. For a moment he was back in the Thompson house, looking at the body of Janet Thompson, bloody, brutalized, and left sprawled across a bed like this one.

Dell shuddered.

He shook his head and pushed the memory away. As a lawman, it was his job to stay clear-headed. To take each crime and criminal as they came, not allowing them to cloud his judgment.

That was the way it was supposed to work, at least.

He took a deep breath, tried to refocus on the task at hand. More ropes were tied to the iron bedposts. The outlaw had brought Clare Willows in here, tied her down, and raped her.

Dell grabbed a corner of the bedcovers and shook them. A pocketknife fell out and clunked on the floor. He leaned over and picked it up. It was a fancy one, with a staghorn handle. The blade was still open, but clean — no blood.

This wasn't the murder weapon. Elbert Willows said he'd found the body out on the floor by the front door, and Dell had seen the blood there when he'd first entered the house. The killer had used the pocket-knife to cut her free after the rape, then dragged her out to the front room trying to force her to tell them where the money was hidden. When she hadn't given it up, he'd gutted her, probably with a hunting knife, if her wounds were anything to go by.

Bastard.

The scene had yielded more than most of the crimes he'd solved in the past — three good clues that confirmed the killer wasn't someone who'd belonged here. And that told him Elbert Willows hadn't killed his young wife in a fit of rage, after all.

The dogs barked outside. Pocketing the knife, he retraced his steps out to the porch.

Three men on horseback rode up into the yard. Dell recognized them immediately — Ruff Delaney and his two teenage sons, Buck and Easton, from on down the road a piece.

Ruff reined up, frowning as he saw Dell emerge from the house.

"Afternoon, Sheriff."

Dell tipped his hat. "Howdy, Ruff."

"What brings you out this way? Something happen?"

"Someone murdered Clare Willows here

yesterday."

"Clare? Why would someone do that?"

"Elbert suspects they heard they had money here and came to steal it. Looks like she never told them where, though, even with the bad things they did to her. He said the money's still where they hid it."

The three dismounted. The younger boy looked sick.

Ruff shook his head. "Clare was a nice lady. Made him a good wife. Joined our church and everything. My wife'll be sick to hear about this."

"You boys keep a secret real good?"

"Sure, Dell. What do you need?"

"I don't want a word said, but I found a knife in the house." He dug it out and showed it to them. "Ever seen it before? Know who it belonged to?"

They looked hard at it, then stepped back.

"Can't recall that I ever seen anyone with a knife like that before," Ruff said. "And I think I'd remember if 'n I did."

"Fancy one," Buck, the younger boy, muttered in agreement.

"Don't tell a soul I have it."

"That belong to her killer?" Easton asked.

"It may," Dell said. "But you breathe a word about it and he may run off 'fore I can catch him."

The boy's eyes widened, but he nodded. He asked them if they'd seen any strangers about or noticed anything odd. None of them spoke up, but promised to keep on the lookout for anything out of the ordinary. They also promised to comfort Willows. He was a good neighbor, and they knew he'd be devastated with the loss of his wife. Finally, Dell said his goodbyes, closed up the house, and rode home.

It was near sundown when he rode up and put his horse in the stall for the night. Guinn joined him in the alleyway as he removed the saddle and drew a pail of water. They shared a hug and a kiss. Nice to be home.

"Learn much up there?" she asked as they headed in the back door.

"I know the killer's shoe size and I've got his jackknife."

"Wow, you did good."

"More clues than usual," he agreed. "I find the owner of this knife, he'll have lots to explain."

"Your supper is in the oven. You can tell me all about it while you eat."

"You feeling all right?"

The approaching birth of their first-born was becoming more and more apparent by the day.

"Me?" She laughed. "Oh, heavens I feel fine. I'm just too big. He may be three foot tall when he comes out."

"How do you know it won't be a really tall girl?"

"I hope not. I never found a man tall enough for me until I found you."

"We don't know the sex," he said.

"Fussy. I want a boy."

"I want a child we can hug, hold, and help grow up."

"Now that you've got me started, we may have a tribe of them."

"I'm happy with whatever."

"I'll worry about another after this one is here," she said.

Dell pulled her close and wrapped her in his arms. "Guinn, you don't know how neat you are. I thank God for you every day."

"Me too, big man. We were made for each other."

He sat down heavily, shaking his head. What a life he'd picked out to do — but she was there to steer him on. He had thought after losing his first wife he'd never find another. But then Guinn came along, and after the lengthy divorce effort, she'd filled the void like he'd never dreamed anyone could.

TWELVE

The next day, Dell met with Wilbur and the town marshal, Hanks. He showed them the knife and explained where he'd found it. The killer had used it to cut the ropes binding the woman to the bed. Maybe in the struggle, he'd lost it in the covers.

Neither man recognized the blade, but agreed it was not a common knife, and whoever owned it had some questions to answer about where it had been discovered.

"What size were the boot tracks?" Wilbur asked.

"Maybe a seven? I'm not certain, but a lot smaller than mine, and the right one has hole in the sole."

"Well, Dell, you sure do have some evidence on this," Hanks said.

"I really thought Elbert had done it to begin with," Dell admitted. "But what I saw out there leads me to believe it was someone else. They wanted the money. When she didn't give it to them, they raped, tortured, and murdered her."

Wilbur scowled. "Doc said she'd been raped."

"That was a horrible crime. I want the killer."

"You know where to start from here?"

"I've got an idea. Wilbur, you know the men who helped round up the prisoners? I want you to take the knife and show it around, see if they recognize it and who it might belong to. But keep it quiet, and tell them to keep their mouths shut about it."

The deputy nodded. "I can do that."

"Fred, I want you to keep your ears open. Drunk men talk sometimes, blab about things they should keep secret."

"Exactly," Hanks agreed. "I'll be listening for someone to let something slip."

"What do you intend to do, Dell?" Wilbur asked.

"Talk to Elbert's neighbors. They may know more than we do. Someone heard about the money they kept in the house and made a go at it. Elbert said he'd mentioned something about not trusting banks to a bunch he was playing poker with a while back. I'd like the names of those men he was playing cards with. Lots to look into, though. Tomorrow I'll ride back out early and start talking to the neighbors. Turn your thinking on, we need to solve this murder."

"Funeral is this afternoon," Wilbur reminded him.

Dell put on his hat as he headed out the door. "Guinn and I will be there. That's why I'm going back tomorrow instead of starting today."

Borrowing a buckboard and team from the livery, Dell loaded his wife up for the drive out to the cemetery. She teased him about the rig most of the way there.

"Oh, I guess if we were gad-abouts I'd buy us a team like this and buckboard of our own."

"You've got a big, fat wife and a baby on the way. You don't think we need one now?"

He shook his head. "One more thing to fuss over. Sometimes you'd have to feed the horses when I was gone."

"I could do that."

He grinned. "Okay, Missus Hoffman. I'll consider buying a rig."

"Good decision." She hugged his arm.

"Nagged me into it."

Guinn smacked him on the shoulder. "I don't nag you."

"Only sometimes."

"When it's important."

"You're always important to me."

"Good," she smiled. "If you still love me now, when I get back to my old body, you can love me more."

He shook his head, guiding the team around another wagon in the road. "Boy, oh boy, you are after me today."

"You know I treasure every day we share."

"I say the same thing."

"Lots of people here today," she said as they neared the cemetery and spied the crowd gathering there.

"Good. Poor Elbert's sick over losing her."

"How old was she?" Guinn asked under her breath.

"Fifteen, sixteen maybe."

"See? I bet you could have found an even younger wife."

Dell snorted. "No thanks."

"Good," she said as he helped her down from the rig.

Several of the town's women surrounded them, making a fuss over her growing belly. Dell gently passed her over into their care and told her he'd be back in a minute. He saw a rancher who lived out near the Willows' place and wanted to ask him a few questions.

"Hurry back, my love," Guinn said with a smile.

Troy Reams was in his fifties, with graying

sideburns and deep blue eyes that didn't miss much of anything. He owned the Bar O ranch, and Dell had known him for a decade or more. They shook hands and talked about the weather for a few minutes before Dell asked about the murder.

"You have any earthly idea who might have killed this poor girl, Troy?"

Reams looked pained. "Dell, I've been thinking about it since the moment I heard. You have any leads?"

"Just a few slim ones." He dug into his pocket and pulled out the pocketknife. "You ever see this before?"

The rancher took the knife and held it up in the light, looking it over carefully. "Looks familiar. You find it there?"

Dell nodded. "It was open in the bed covers. I think the killer had her tied on the bed and used it to cut the ropes off, then lost it scuffling around with her."

"Did they —"

"Yes. Doc confirmed she'd been raped."

Reams shook his head and handed the knife back over. "Animals. How can people do things like this?"

"I should've expected it after I saw the body, no more respect than they had for her — cutting her all up like that. Elbert said he told some men in a card game he didn't use banks because of things like the robbery we had a while back."

"That would have been bait, all right," Reams agreed.

"I found some footprints at the scene. Whoever did it has a boot size smaller than either of us."

"Anything else besides the knife and tracks?"

"Nothing."

"Looks like the service is starting." From across the way, they heard the preacher's voice rise above the chatter of the crowd, but Reams stopped Dell from moving with a hand on his arm. "Clare Willows was a beautiful and kind young woman, Dell. This can't go unpunished. Anything I can do to help, you let me know."

The funeral was a sad affair for all involved. Willows sobbed so loudly even the women had become uncomfortable, wishing silently for the preacher to finish his eulogy. Finally, after paying their respects, Dell was able to guide Guinn away and load her back up into the buckboard.

"Nice service," he said. "Who were the women with Elbert?"

"I'm not sure. It wasn't her people, though. They were the loud bunch across from us." She shrugged. "Wait. No, I know.

The lightheaded one was his sister, and the other lady was some relative, too. They came from San Angelo."

"See?" He laughed. "You know more than me."

"Missus Armstrong told me before the funeral. I just forgot." She winced. "I'll be glad when this baby gets here. Pregnancy is making me dumb."

"Hush, now. You're thinking for three people these days. You have cause to be forgetful."

Guinn looked confused. "Three?"

"You, the baby, and me."

She laughed so hard, she almost wet herself.

"So you're still feeling good? This was all right?"

"Anywhere I can go with you is fine," she said. "We don't have to hide anymore."

"Oh, yes," he agreed. "It's much better."

"Even if you got a divorced woman?"

"I'm simply pleased to have you."

"And such a big woman."

"All of that."

They both laughed.

Making certain she was safe in the house, he took the rig back to the livery. Rob Perlman, the owner, laughed when he said he'd need one of his own and a team to go with it.

"I'll keep my eye out for a bargain for ya, Dell."

"Good. It'll have to be a bargain for me to afford it."

"You can have that one anytime, no charge. You know I appreciate what you do for all of us."

"You do good enough now keeping my horse handy and feeding him," he said.

"No problem. You figure out who killed Clare Willows?"

"Not yet." Dell shook his head and reached in his pocket. "You ever seen this knife?"

Perlman squinted and looked it over carefully. "Nah. That what they cut her up with?"

"No. Doc and I figure they used a big knife for that. They lost this one open-bladed in the bed covers."

"Ah, shit." The livery owner spat in disgust. "They raped her, too?"

"Doc says so."

"I hope you can find him, Dell," Perlman said. "We need that sumbitch hung."

The anger in the man's voice made Dell's blood run cold.

THIRTEEN

It had been a rough night. Guinn had tossed and turned, unable to get comfortable around the bulk of the baby growing in her belly. As for him, thoughts of Clare Willows's murder kept swirling through his head, bloody images flashing before his eyes like bad memories. Around 4:30, they'd both finally given in and gotten up. Now Guinn was down in the kitchen making breakfast, as he prepared to face another morning in search of a brutal murderer on the loose.

The people in town were angry. Angry and scared. The talks he'd had with people before and after the funeral had been more than enough to convince him of that. They'd been on edge ever since the night of the Thompson killings and bank robbery, but this new murder had everybody near ready to stampede. He had to get the killer — and fast.

Dell sat on the bed and pulled on his boots. He was out there now, the man who had killed Clare Willows — somewhere in the darkness. Surely he'd realized by now that he'd left something behind, a clue that could be traced back to him with very little effort. He'd have to be stupid not to. Eventually, someone would recognize the knife, and the hole in the boot sole would convict him beyond the shadow of a doubt. The question was, would he do anything about it? Would he go so far as to go back to the scene of the crime and look for it? Maybe, maybe not. But if the loss of the knife had the unknown man upset, it was a good thing — a damn good thing. Desperate men made mistakes, missed things when trying to cover their tracks. And when he did, Dell would be there.

At breakfast, Guinn told him that Nan, her sister, would be coming over to spend the day with her. That was a relief. She was close enough to term he'd begun to worry constantly about her going into labor all alone while he was at the jail or out on a case. Nan would keep an eye on her in his absence, keep everything calm.

He ran into several folks on the way to the jail, and but one thing was one all their minds — Clare Willows. He hadn't even walked out his own garden gate when his next-door neighbor, Mrs. Walker, waved him down to talk about it. She and her husband Ezra were shocked by the crime. How could another brutal murder like that happen in their little town?

Tim Plummer, the clerk at the town's assay office, rode by in his buggy and waved hello. He was just as upset as the Walkers, and worried about the safety of his own wife and daughters. His wife had even brought up the subject of moving up toward Dallas to get away from all the violence here.

Dell had lunch with Rosie White, a bright rancher's widow in her seventies who lived near the Willows place. She set a nice table and made a fuss about his coming by. She wanted to know all about Guinn and the baby coming, but knew nothing of value related to the murder.

Weed Briggs stopped him on the road back to town. He was mounted on a gun-shy, watch-eyed horse he was trying to break to ride. The horse circled around impatiently, causing Briggs to jerk him down every so often.

"Hey, Dell. Guess you're looking for Clare's killer, huh?"

"Him and maybe more."

"Damn bad business." Briggs shook his

head. "Clare was a sweet girl. God rest her soul, but she was some wild before she married old Willows."

"They say she went pretty straight after her marriage."

"Yeah, but a couple of 'em bitched about her being ungrateful. She wasn't about to give them any more and ran them off."

This piece of information interested Dell. "You hear things I don't. Who said that?"

"Don't tell them I told you, but that Ramsey boy bragged some about having her. Tillman Jointer said she'd really changed from the old girl he ran around with before she got married."

"Hey, get that horse broke. He's a good-looking pony save for that watch eye."

"Some folks think that's lucky." Briggs laughed, patting the horse's flank. "But he damn sure can run."

With a nod and thanks, Dell rode off thinking about the two young men mentioned. It wasn't Jointer's bootprint at the hitching rail — that boy wore boots bigger than Dell's. But what about Earnest Ramsey? He was a short, cocky boy of about nineteen who Dell wouldn't trust going out with anyone's daughter, let alone his own. Bet he had small feet too.

He reined Burt to a halt. Where could he

find that boy? The Ramseys had a cattle operation out west of Temple Hill, a small peak they said the Comanches had built signal fires on that had become a sacred place for the red men — thus the name. He cut across country and reached the Ramsey place about four o'clock. He found Mrs. Ramsey sweeping the rock-floored porch and shooing chickens away with a large straw broom. She looked up and smiled as he approached.

"What can I do for you, Sheriff?"

"Afternoon, Mae. Your boy Earnest around?"

"You want him?"

"I'd like to talk to him, if I could."

"You sure can," she said. "He got back late last night from a horse-buying trip and is sleeping in the backyard on a hammock. I'll go wake him."

Dell dismounted and stretched his legs. "I'll go along."

"How's your wife? I hear you two are having a baby soon?" She looked back at him, shading her eyes against the sun. "What will you call it?"

"We're not certain yet."

Mrs. Ramsey laughed. "Well, naming babies is always fun to argue over."

They rounded the corner of the house into

229

the backyard. Young Ramsey lay snoring in a hammock strung between two poplars swaying gently in the breeze. His hat, belt, pants, and boots lay piled on the ground nearby. While Mae bent over to wake her son, Dell bent over and picked up one of the boots. It was small, a size seven. Then he turned it over and looked at the sole.

"The sheriff is here, Earnest," she was telling the boy. "He wants to talk to you, dear."

"Thanks, Ma." Earnest Ramsey struggled upright in the hammock and squinted in the afternoon sun. He looked bleary-eyed, like he was coming off a bad drunk. "What do you need, Sheriff?"

Dell held out the boot in his hand. "This yours?"

"Yes it is one of mine." The boy's gaze darted back and forth between his mother and Dell. "Why?"

"It's got a hole in the sole."

"So?"

"I found tracks from this boot at the Willows house the day Clare was murdered," Dell said, trying to control the anger in his voice.

Mrs. Ramsey gasped. "Oh, Earnest!"

"No, Ma! I can explain! Please!" Earnest struggled to his feet, all but falling out of the hammock in his haste. "Listen. I never killed Clare, Sheriff, I loved her. Yes, I was having an affair with her, I admit, but I could never hurt her. She'd finally come back to her senses and planned to leave Willows, I swear to God."

"Where's your pocketknife?" Dell demanded.

The boy shook his head. "Huh? I sure never cut her up like they said. She was in one piece and fine when I left her that day."

"Get out your pocketknife," he pressed.

Earnest scooped up his pants and dug into the pocket, coming up with a battered, wood-handled knife rusty around the hinge. "Here's the one dad bought me in Fort Worth a few years back."

Dell snatched the knife away and examined it carefully.

"That's his only one I know about," Mrs. Ramsey said. "Why would you ever think my boy murdered that girl?"

"His boots match the tracks I found in front of the house."

Earnest nodded. "Clare let me know her old man would be gone. We had a signal. She'd leave a bucket upside down up on the post by the road. I rode over there that morning and we had sex. But it was willing, Mister Hoffman, and I wouldn't killed her for anything — we talked about her even leaving him. We talked about it all the time."

"What time did you leave the house?"

"Just before lunch. Her husband wasn't supposed to be back until late, but I had to help Pa fix a fence out on the east end, so I left early." Tears coursed down the boy's face. "But I swear to God I didn't kill her, Sheriff. I loved that woman."

Dell handed the knife back. "Don't leave the county, Earnest. If Billy Lee decides to hold a hearing, you'll have to attend and testify. And if you're lying to me —"

"I'm not, I swear!"

"— I *will* find out, and I *will* lock you up."

"When I heard they killed her —"

"Who's *they*?" Dell shouted.

"Just words. I don't know who done it, or I'd already killed them myself."

He stepped forward and poked the boy in the chest. "You better keep your eyes and ears open, son, because whoever the killer is, he's local. He may have watched you leave. Nobody from outside these parts would know Willows kept all his money hid in that house."

"I'll find the sumbitch who did it," Earnest said through gritted teeth. "I'll find him and slit his gawdam throat."

Mrs. Ramsey put her hand to her breast. "Earnest!"

"You'll do no such thing," Dell said. "If you hear anything, you come find me. I'll take care of it. The killer will hang, I promise, but only after a trial. You understand what I'm saying, son?"

The boy didn't answer.

"Don't make me lock you up for your own good, kid."

"Earnest, answer the Sheriff."

"I understand," he said, his voice sullen.

Dell was still angry as he mounted Burt and rode off. He'd been a lawman for years now, and he had a knack for reading people. Earnest Ramsey was too young to fake the kind of grief and outrage he'd shown over Clare's death. He was a hotheaded kid in love with another man's wife, but he was no murderer.

Damn. That meant half his evidence was gone. Now he had the knife — and more unanswered questions. Clare Willows had obviously gone back to her wild ways and resumed entertaining men other than her husband. Had she loved Ramsey like the boy had thought, or had he just been one pleasant diversion among many? Dell couldn't say yet, but the jilted lover angle still didn't sit right in his craw. His gut told him this was about money, not love or sex. He needed to —

Dell heard the crack of a gunshot and felt Burt stumble beneath him. Without thinking, he shook his feet out of the stirrups and threw himself off the mount. He hit the sandy ground hard on his shoulder as the horse fell behind him with an awful shriek.

Dell rolled to his feet and bolted, bullets kicking up spurts of dust close by his flying boots. A copse of cedar rose out of the rocks ahead. He ran that way, dodging and weaving between the shots. Crashing through the gummy evergreen bows, he dropped to his belly and drew his pistol, trying to orient himself toward where the shooters were firing at him from.

Burt lay back in the dust where he'd fallen, silent and unmoving. Dell ground his molars tighter, anger surging through him once again. Whoever they were, the bastards had killed his damned horse.

He stopped when he heard a horse being pushed through the trees toward him. A simple face and hat appeared out of the brush, and Dell raised his gun. In an instant he got a quick shot off as the man emerged from the cedars. His bullet struck the rider in the face, and the horse bucked him off.

How many more were out there waiting? He needed to change places. Single shots were always hard to locate. He could move over to where the boughs were taller and listen for movement.

Dell moved to his left, straining to hear voices or another horse, the needles sticking to his clothes. The sharp, pungent smell of cedar assaulted his nose and settled bitter on his tongue. The one he'd shot had jumped the gun, wading into the cedar copse and paying the price for his clumsiness. More must be nearby, waiting for him to show himself — and if they had any brains at all, they wouldn't give him another chance like that one did.

He waited there in the cedars for a long time, but heard nothing more. Either there had only been one shooter, after all, or the others had run off. Whichever had happened, though, he couldn't just sit here any longer.

Moving quietly, he edged toward the edge of the brush and peeked out toward the road. He saw nothing but the outlaw's body, lying facedown in the shallow ruts of the trail. Keeping low, he headed that way, pistol out and ready.

Dell knelt beside the still form and felt for a pulse. Nothing at the wrist, or the neck.

He rolled the man over and checked the face — what was left of it, at least. Dell's single .45 bullet had caught him just below the left eye and blown out the back of his head. He wasn't anybody Dell could place right off, though. Rough looking feller. Probably mid-twenties, unshaven, with shabby hair and clothes dusted brown from the trail. Nothing but a few dollars and some chaw in one pocket. His six-gun looked well cared for, but really, he looked like nothing more than some cowpoke riding the chuckline looking for work.

Disgusted, Dell stood and holstered his pistol. He picked up the dead man's arms and drug him far enough off the road so a wagon could pass and not run him over. He'd send the boy from the funeral home out here to get the corpse once he got back to town.

He snorted. *If* he ever got back. With Burt gone, it would be a hell of a long walk.

Wait. The shooter had been mounted when Dell had hit him. Where had his horse gotten off to in the meantime?

He found it in a meadow a small stretch farther up the road, head down, grazing in the wild grass. The bay threw its head up at his approach, but stayed put, eyeing him suspiciously. Moving slowly, Dell caught the reins and pulled the gelding in, speaking calming words and rubbing his snout. He carried a bedroll and a pair of saddlebags behind the worn saddle, and an empty scabbard for a rifle.

Overcome with curiosity, he decided to go ahead and check the saddlebags. He found food in one, letters in another, all addressed in the name of Clay Hooten. All but the one on top were from the guy's mother, who looked to live up close to the Indian Territory line. But the other one. . . .

Dear Clay,

They tell me you need work. I have some for you. Kill Sheriff Hoffman of Saddler County, Texas and I'll pay you four hundred dollars. All I need is the newspaper story covering it mailed to me at Box 34 Las Vegas, New Mexico,

Rollo Magnus

Rollo Magnus.

Wasn't that something. So his wanted man hadn't gone as far as he thought he had — and he still had Dell on his mind, too. Wasn't that flattering? Dell would have to make sure someone payed Rollo a nice visit. Someone like a US Deputy Marshal to arrest him and bring him back to Texas for trial.

Thanks, Clay. For this goosey horse, too.

It was late when he got back to the house.

237

Guinn was waiting up for him and brought a lamp out to the barn.

"What did you fall into?" she asked, wrinkling her nose.

"Had to wallow around under some cedar trees today. This isn't Burt, either. The man owned him shot Burt, which really made me mad. He isn't among the living now. I'll send the undertaker after his body in the morning."

"You lost your good Steel Dust horse?"

"Missed me and shot Burt. I loved that old horse." He shook his head as she patted his shoulder. "I also learned more about Clare's murder."

"You can tell me all about it later." She kissed him, and they walked toward the house hand in hand. "I have food in the oven and I can heat some water for you for a bath."

"You're an angel."

"I might be an avenging angel with how bad you look. Who shot at you?"

"Some kid from up Indian Territory way. I was riding down the road near Temple Hill when he started firing. He hit Burt with the first shot and spilled me on the ground. I got under some cedars, and when he came blundering through after me, I shot him and sent him to the devil." He shook his head.

"He had no help. But that's not the important part. Guess who hired him?"

"Who?"

"Rollo Magnus."

Her eyes widened. "The one who —"

"Yep." Dell nodded. "The address he gave the kid was in Las Vegas."

"By hired, you mean . . . he paid the man to kill you?"

"Looks that way."

"Dell, what are you going to do?"

"Send a Deputy US Marshal to go arrest him."

"That easy?"

He nodded and helped her up the steps. "That easy."

She stopped him on the back porch. "This is terrible. I'm so glad you made it back."

"So am I."

"Who else did he hire?"

Dell shrugged. "Lord only knows."

"You better get someone to ride with you from here on." Her tone made it clear the point wasn't up for argument.

"Yes ma'am." He nodded. "But how will I pay him? The county is broke since the bank got robbed."

"You'll find a way," she said. "But you're not to go out riding alone like that again until this is resolved."

"I'll try, my dear."

"You'll do more than try, Delbert. Now shed those clothes out here. No one will see you and I don't want all those sticky needles in my house."

"Easy enough. Here, take my gun belt."

After his supper and bath, he felt much better and they turned in. Next morning after breakfast, he walked to the office.

After the excitement of yesterday, he'd hoped for a quiet day. But there in the early morning sun outside his jail were three horses. One had a body across it, the other wore Dell's saddle, and the last a fine leather saddle of its own.

Jogging up the steps to the boardwalk, he yanked open the door and walked inside. Behind the desk, Wilbur jumped up from his chair in surprise.

"Dell!"

"Mornin', Wilbur."

"Where have you been, Boss? Everything okay? I was fixing to get a party up to look for you. Jim Campbell found a body and your dead horse up on the Slyder Road about dark last night."

"Thanks, Jim." Dell shook the rancher's hand. "You know the dead man?"

"No, sir," Campbell said. "It was right at sunset when I found him. Then I stumbled across the horse and recognized your rig. I went looking for you, but by that time it was so dark, I couldn't hardly see my hand in front of my face. So I went home to get another horse and came back for the body and your saddle. Then I caught a few hours' sleep and headed in here at first light, dreading that he'd shot you and left you for dead out in the cedars."

"I shot him after he shot Burt. Caught his horse and rode him on in, got home long after dark. I'd planned to send the funeral home after his body this morning."

"Who was he?" Wilbur asked.

"A guy named Clay Hooten. Our old friend Rollo Magnus hired him to shoot me. That devil's living out in Las Vegas, and I'm wiring the US Marshals there to arrest him today."

"Jim," Wilbur said, "Magnus's the guy behind the murders and bank robbery a few months back."

"Oh, my God. You're lucky to be alive, Dell."

"Naw, this guy was a piss-poor shot."

Wilbur shook his head in disbelief.

Dell didn't laugh. "My scrambling under those sticky cedars saved my life. Until they arrest this damn killer, Guinn says I can't go anywhere else on my own. And I'll need another horse. I'll damn sure miss that gelding of mine."

Jim spoke up. "Me and my neighbors will bury your pony up there. I know you have lots to do, and we can at least do that for you."

Dell swallowed hard. "Burt was a fine animal. You don't get but a few horses or dogs you really like everything about them. I did that with him. Had him for five years, never had a bad day, never had a sick or lame day, got along with other horses fine. He never pitched me off or tried that hard. I've been feeling sorry for myself ever since he went down. I won't find another like him easy. But tell everyone I'm better at managing the law for them than digging a grave. Thank them for me, too."

"Sheriff Hoffman!" a boy from down the street burst into the jail, breathing hard.

"Yes, boy? What's wrong?"

"They've called for the midwife. Your woman is springing."

It took Dell a moment to understand what the boy meant. Springing — most folks said that about cows. But right now, the kid was talking about Guinn. She was having the baby.

Guinn was having the baby!

Dell shook Jim's hand, told Wilbur to

handle things, and headed for the door.

"Dell?"

He stopped to look back.

"Want me to send that wire to Las Vegas about Magnus?" Wilbur asked him.

"Good thinking. I got more important things to worry about right now. Thanks, partner." Then he walked out.

"I'm praying for ten toes and ten fingers and healthy lungs, Dell!" his deputy shouted after him.

Fourteen

Babies come when they get damn good and ready. The clock struck eleven p.m., and still no baby.

Nan and Ralph Stafford were with him. This was their baby, too. In six years of marriage, they'd never been able to conceive. Guinn and Nan were closer than most sisters, too. When Howard ran off on Guinn, she had to move in with them.

That's how she and Dell had met. Ralph was the town's saddlemaker — and a good one — and he and Dell had known one another for years. They'd invited him over for supper. While he'd known of Guinn for some time, he'd never actually met her until that night. The affair between them had kicked off soon after.

Dell hadn't been interested in finding another wife, but Guinn was so neat and intelligent they'd soon begun to bond. He'd never realized just how hard a divorce was to obtain, though. Without the help and knowledge of his Ranger friends, he and Guinn might still be sneaking around, unmarried, and not pacing around in his parlor waiting on the arrival of their first-born.

Time drug on. Thomas City might not have that new arrival until tomorrow.

Nan patted his knee. "She's doing fine, Dell. Doc Kelton sees no problems. It'll get here soon."

"He and Donna Lacey deliver a lot of babies," Ralph agreed. "Donna's the best midwife around."

The clock struck midnight, and then at one minute past the hour, they heard a baby cry.

Nan went into the birthing room to check on things. She came back with a tiny boy.

He had no idea how big or small the boy was — he was simply there. Filled with a joy the likes of which he'd never known, Dell cradled his son close and gave a silent prayer of thanks. Still carrying the child, he walked slowly back to the lower bedroom — the room he and his first wife had slept in. Guinn and Nan had gotten it all ready to have the baby in there. When she'd asked if he minded, he'd told her, "Lord no. This is your house. We used the upstairs so no one could see what we were doing." She'd laughed and pushed him away, waggling a naughty finger. What a neat slice of life they had together so far — and now the child was there.

She sat upright in the birthing bed, looking like she were waiting for him. She smiled tiredly as he walked through the door. She looked exhausted, but beautiful. Angelic. Because that's what she was, his angel. She and the baby.

"Hello, Dell," she said in a low voice. "Look what we did."

Dell rocked the bundle in his arms and smiled back. "It's a blessing, Guinn. You both are. The greatest ones I've ever had."

"And you're mine."

"What should we call him?" he asked.

"Teddy, I think."

"Not Theodore?" Guinn had once mentioned she flat refused to tie any child — boy or girl — down to two names like poor Billy Lee.

"No, just Teddy Hoffman. No middle name or these Texans will call him that. And Theodore's not a name for him. Anyone calls you Delbert, you about choke, so why scar him with such a long-handle name?"

He laughed, then bent over and kissed her still-damp forehead. "Nan wants to stay here with you tonight. I told her she could. This was an emotional time for her."

"I know how she feels," Guinn said. "I've been at other births and wondered why I couldn't have one, too. Thanks for thinking of her."

"Do I need to do anything for you?"

"Take Ralph upstairs and put him to bed in the other bedroom. He'll want to be up early like you. Buy him breakfast at the café. You two deserve it. Us girls will keep Teddy here and spoil him rotten."

"I believe that's just what you'll do, too." Very carefully, Dell handed Teddy off into his mother's arms. It was the most beautiful thing he'd ever seen.

With the baby tucked carefully to her breast, she looked back up at him. "What will you do about a horse?"

He shook his head. "Don't worry about me. Perlman will find me one."

"Don't you get yourself shot."

"Yes, mother."

She smiled again. "You and him are all I have, Dell. I'm never not going to worry."

He kissed her one more time, then went to awaken Ralph, who was dozing on the sofa. They trudged up the stairs, and Dell set the alarm clock for six. After a short night, they dressed and walked down town to have breakfast, telling everyone they saw that Guinn had delivered a healthy baby boy they'd named Teddy. It was as if the boy had two proud papas.

At four o'clock that afternoon, Wayne Sellers brought a hat full of money to him in the office. Paper money, coins, Mexican and American, he poured it out on the desk in front of Dell with a grin that stretched from ear to ear.

"Folks call it the Horse Fund. There's one hundred fifteen dollars and twenty-seven cents, Dell. It came from lots of folks rich and poor. They all wanted to help replace your old Steel Dust pony. All of us appreciate what you do around here."

"What?" Dell gasped. "Why, Wayne, this town is broke. That may be all the cash people have. I can't take that."

"Yes, you can," Sellers said. "Our lawman went to west Texas with no expenses paid and got most of the outlaws who robbed us blind. You were out looking for another killer when you got your horse shot out from under you. You did that for us. This ain't nothing but heartfelt money for you."

Dell put the money in the bottom desk drawer and closed it. "I can't say thanks enough. I have a new son today, too. We called him Teddy."

"That's great," Sellers agreed. "Tell Guinn we love her, too. And that she can expect the ladies of the town to come visit over the next couple of days to pay their respects."

"I will. And I'll find a good new horse you all can be proud of."

Sellers put his hat back on and smiled. "Lost a horse and got a son. Ain't a bad trade."

Rob Perlman came in the door a few minutes later.

"Come out here. I have something to show you," the livery owner said.

Outside, Dell saw a boy ride up on a big sorrel gelding with a flaxen mane and tail. It was a beautiful animal, but with three white stockings and a blaze face, he was sure flashier than any Dell might have chosen. The boy took off running and the horse made sharp strides. Then he stopped and backed him up two lengths.

"Four years old," Perlman said at his side. "What'cha think?"

"More horse than I can afford," Dell laughed.

Perlman shook his head. "You want him he's yours."

"What is this, Free Horse Day?"

Perlman laughed. "Clyde and Roman Thurman from the Box R sent that boy down here with a note that said, 'Give this horse to Sheriff Hoffman. It won't replace that Steel Dust horse but he's handy and proud enough for our sheriff to ride. Box R Ranch.' "

"Wayne Sellers just brought me a hat fund to buy one."

"Save it. They may shoot this one, too."

"Oh, I hope not." Dell shook his head. "I'll take him, though."

"Thought you might. Hey, Polo," he called to the young rider. "Come on down from there. Poppa here has to go home and change a diaper."

"You heard already?"

Perlman nodded. "Be sure to tell Guinn how happy we all are for her."

"I can do that. She's very pleased."

The stable owner clapped him on the shoulder. "I'll bet she is, partner."

He went home and found Ralph peeling potatoes in the kitchen. The women had finally gotten the baby down and were taking a nap. Dell rolled up his sleeves and pitched in, and they had supper ready in just a few minutes. They ate together, trading pages of The Dallas Weekly Herald from the day before, and chose not to bother the women. Before turning in, though, Dell left Guinn a note.

Hello Darling,

Ralph and I didn't want to wake you, so we had supper on our own. I hope you and the baby are fine. Everybody in town wanted me to tell you how happy they are for us. You'll probably be seeing some of the ladies visit over the next day or two. Don't worry about us. We'll eat breakfast in town again tomorrow, and I'll see you when I get home. I have lots to tell you. I love you both, and I can't wait to see you again.

Love,
Dell

He woke once during the night to the sounds of commotion downstairs — the baby crying and hurrying footsteps on hardwood flooring. It took only a minute or two before they had little Teddy quieted down, though, and he went right back to sleep. It was sure going to be a different world sharing their life with a baby.

Fifteen

In the morning, Dell rode up to see if the range war had cooled between the Circle H and the Emerson bunch yet. He swung by the Circle H first and found the crew all out. The wife of the foreman, Twain Carpenter, said they were cutting out some culls and had everyone up on the north end of the ranch.

"Has there been any more trouble up here with the Emerson family?" he asked.

"Not nothing real serious," she said. "They drove a bunch of our cows and calves back down here and said we'd crowded over on 'em. Twain told them to put up a fence, cows went where they wanted to go on free open range. But nothing else came of it."

"So no more fights?"

"No." But the look on her face told him there was more to the story.

"Ola, tell me straight. Did they get in a fight?"

She shook her head. "No, but they wanted one. Twain says they're crazy. He made all his hands sit still and let them rant and rave until they's done. They finally just left."

"Thanks. Tell Twain that was the way to handle it. I appreciate it."

"You know he ain't here all the time," she warned. "They come pull that and he ain't here, them cowboys of his may not take it."

"Let's just have peace for now," Dell said. "Plenty of grass and range out there."

"Tell them that. They started it the first time and keep trying to do it again."

"I bet they have another story."

"Well, it's who you believe."

He frowned. "I don't doubt what you tell me, but the shoe on the other foot will usually say the opposite. Let's try to cut this war business down. Someone will get killed before long if we don't."

"Twain did his part."

"Damn right he did. Thank him for me." Dell tipped his hat. "Thanks, Ola. I'm going over and say the same thing to the Emersons."

"How's that new boy of yours?"

"He sure has lungs." He laughed.

"Good. Tell Guinn I said hi. She's a good woman for you."

"More than I deserve," he agreed.

"Thanks again."

Two hours later, Dell rode up the long driveway toward the Emerson headquarters when a rifle-armed cowboy stopped him a quarter mile short of the house.

"What's your business here?"

"I'm the Sheriff of this county." He pulled his vest back and showed him the badge on his shirt. "My name's Dell Hoffman."

The man pulled out a small notebook and thumbed through it. When he didn't find what he was looking for, he stuffed it back in his shirt pocket. "You ain't on the list."

"Pardon me?"

The man swung the rifle barrel around and pointed his way. "You can't go up there."

Dell narrowed his eyes at the man. "Who gives you orders, son?" he asked in a quiet voice.

"Tom Emerson. The man who owns the ranch."

"I know Tom. I know his sons. I'm the Sheriff in this county, and I want to talk to them."

The guard wasn't impressed. "Well, if your name ain't on my list and you try to go past me, I'll shoot you. We've been raided more than once and had half our haystacks burned. One of Mister Emerson's boys even got a leg broken. If'n I let you by, I'll get fired. So turn around and go away."

Dell raised his hands in surrender. "All right, all right, son. When you go in tonight, you tell Tom and those two boys the sheriff was out here and you refused him entry. Tell him I said he has twenty-four hours to report to me at the jail, or I'll get a search warrant and a posse out here and see everything I want."

"He won't do that."

"Fine. He don't, and I'll come see him with the authority." He reined the new horse around and went back to town.

Every mile of the way he thought more about that guard. He was not some ordinary cowboy, but another of those *pistoleros* — a hired gun like Rollo Magnus had employed. And where one went, there were sure to be more. Why in the hell did Tom Emerson have such men on his payroll? To cause trouble? Or to back him against his neighbors with a more powerful force?

Burned haystack, huh? Probably some clumsy smoker did that with a discarded match and blamed the neighbors to cover his mistake.

This entire thing had gone far enough. He'd stop it when he met with Tom.

Back at the jail, he gave a young boy a

dime to take his horse to the livery — told him they would know what to do with him. Resetting his gun out of habit, he pushed on inside the jail.

Wilbur looked up from some paperwork. "What's got you so upset?"

Dell took a deep breath. "I talked to Twain's wife Ola down at Circle H — they were all gone. She said Emerson's drove cows and calves over saying they'd crowded 'em onto their land, then tried to start a fight. I rode over to the Emersons and some hired gun stopped me short of the house. Said I wasn't on the accepted list of visitors and refused me entry."

Wilbur made a face. "You mean you never even got to talk to them?"

"No. But I told that damn ringy if Tom and them boys didn't report to me at the jail within twenty-four hours, I was coming back with a posse and a warrant and examining everything they had."

"What the hell was wrong with him?"

"Tom can damn sure come in here and explain it to me, or I'm riding back and giving him holy hell."

"I haven't seen you this mad in a long time."

"This whole range war is stupid." Dell spat. "Ola told me Twain had to make his men stand back and not answer Emerson's threats. Tom better get his ass in here and explain his new road guard preventing me from talking to him."

"Think I ought to stick around a while?" Wilbur asked.

"No, go home. He knows where I live."

"How was your new horse?"

"He was good. But if I'd still had Burt, I'd've spurred him right into that guard and unseated him." He frowned. "This horse might have done it, but he's untested."

Dell went home when the night jail guard arrived. Back at the house, he found Guinn rattling around in the kitchen with the baby in a crib nearby.

She smiled broadly. "Daddy's home, Teddy!"

He leaned in for a kiss, then went to the crib for a look.

"You have a good day?" she asked.

"Not at all," he said. "I went to see about that damn range war and a guard at Tom Emerson's gate refused me admittance."

"Why'd he do that?"

"He had a list and told me I wasn't on it."

"So what are you going to do?"

"I sent him word he needs to come see me in twenty-four hours, or I'd take a posse up there and force my way through."

"You sound mad," she said.

"I'm trying to settle that war up there before someone is killed."

"I hope you can eat. I fixed ham and yams like you like them."

Dell sighed. "Darling, I'm not mad at you or the boy. It's the stupid grownups that don't know any better. I'm pleased to be here with you."

"Wash up and we can eat."

"I'll do that." He hung up his holster on the wall peg. "Tell me why are people so thick-headed?"

"To get their own ways about things."

"I guess you're right." He shook his head as he washed. "But I'll house all the trouble-makers in my jail before this thing breaks into a shooting war."

She sat him down and kissed him. "You'll work it out. I know you will."

"I wish I was as confident as you. These range wars flare up all over the west and innocent people get hurt and killed."

"I never knew your job was this complex." She put her skirt under her and moved the chair up to the table.

"I love you, Guinn. I hate to bring all this trash home to you and Teddy." The food on the table looked mouth-watering. Smelled like it, too.

"No, I am here as your partner. The baby doesn't have ears yet, but we can tell him the difference when he needs to know. Besides," she said, "if you can't talk to me about these things, why have me?"

"I know we have a better relationship than letting that happen. I get mad at times — not at you, but people like this who start wars to get their demands met."

"That's why you're sheriff, Dell. People expect you to do that and you do a good job. Who else would have gone to El Paso and solved the biggest crime in Texas history?"

"That was yesterday," he growled. "Today some folks are trying to start a range war."

She reached out and squeezed his arm. "Eat supper."

"How did you and Teddy do today?"

"Just fine. Nan went home. She's so much help. But I can see right now she's going to spoil him rotten. I knew she would, but we all need to be spoiled sometimes, don't we?"

"Like you?"

She laughed. "Oh, Dell, what we have is so wonderful including our son. You'll solve the problem with these dummies out there. I have a pecan pie I made special for you today."

"You trying to spoil me?"

259

"You bet I am."

"Thanks. I appreciate it."

"Good. You know I thought my life was over when Howard ran off. It would be tough enough for a woman with children. But a woman married five years without children would never be considered as a wife for a man who wanted a family. He left me nothing. No money. No job. No hope. Nan and Ralph helped me — but you came to my rescue, and now we have Teddy. I am so grateful to have him and you." She rose up and went over to hug his head to her. "I know you know all about my feelings but I am so grateful for this union we share."

Damn, he loved her . . . in all this mess he had an island to rest on. *Thank God for her.*

Sixteen

Tom Emerson and his youngest son Adrian rode into town about nine the next morning. They dismounted in front of the jail and hitched their horses at the rack. Dell saw them from the open door and made a quick appraisal. The man either came to tell him off, or solve this problem for once and for all.

"Dell, I hear you came to see me and my guard wouldn't let you in?"

"I met the man and he refused me admission. I'm the law in this county whether you like it or not, and refusing me entry looks like you've got something to hide."

Emerson twisted his hat brim in his hands. "I never thought about you wanting to see me, or I'd have put you on the list."

"You see this badge I wear?" He pointed to his deputy. "Wilbur, show him your badge, too. These are keys to open any gate. You tell those pie eaters working for you that we can ride in anytime, or you'll start paying the price."

"No need to be mad," Emerson said. "It was my mistake. He was only obeying my orders. I swear it won't happen again."

Dell held up two fingers half an inch apart. "I came that close to knocking him off that horse, Tom. Now this business of your driving cattle over to the Circle H and threatening them has to stop. If you don't have your property fenced, the open range freedom allows those cattle to come eat in your yard."

Emerson frowned, folded his arms. "You taking up for that big outfit over a family rancher?"

"I'm simply saying we have open range in Texas. If it's not fenced, rich or poor, range livestock can graze there."

"Well, I don't agree, gawdammit! Them big outfits aren't running over me."

Dell shook his head. "Tom, don't push this. You can face a fine and a prison sentence if you drive cattle intentionally off land you don't own or is unfenced."

"Well I don't give a damn. Come arrest me. No jury in this county will find me guilty."

"This isn't the old days. You show out and I'll arrest you and any family member involved."

The older man puffed out his chest. "Then you better not come to my ranch ever again."

Dell stiffened. "You better think about that statement, partner. I can get a warrant to search your ranch at any time. This damn range war you're trying to start ends now, do you understand? You don't back down, start acting like a real neighbor to folks, you'll deal with me, and it won't be pleasant. And you also better send those gun hands you've hired on down the road, or I'll start doing it for you. We don't need them in this county."

"Who're you calling a gun hand?"

"That man I met on guard at your gate ain't no ranch hand. He's a hired gun. He doesn't leave, I'll do some investigating into his past. We don't need more strangers in these parts stirring up trouble." Dell stepped to within an inch of the older man, poked a stiff finger into his chest. "I know how range wars start, and I don't want it to happen here. I don't know how many you've hired, but none of 'em better be wanted, or I will charge you with aiding and abetting them."

Emerson didn't back down. "You can't tell me who I hire."

"Tom, I don't think you understand what

I'm saying," he said. "I'm not allowing a range war in this county. That's all there is to it. Clean up your act and get off that high horse. You fire one shot, and I'll throw the lot of you in the pokey."

"Listen, these big outfits are running all over me and I can protect my property. Can and will."

"Not by starting a damn range war."

"You can't —"

Dell shook his head. "Tom. You've heard what I am going to do. Get those gunmen off your payroll — or else."

"I am not taking this sitting down. I'll get you out of this office at the next election."

"You can try. I'm not afraid of your threats or political efforts. I will not allow you to start a range war in my county. Clear out all those gun hands, or I'll clean them out for you."

Emerson's face had turned a bright shade of red. "You can't —"

"Tom leave this jail until you can talk sensible," he said, lowering his voice. "Leave now before you can't."

Emerson turned on his heel and stomped out. His son just stood there for a moment, looking unsure of himself, before he followed.

When he was certain they were gone, Dell

264

turned to Wilbur. "We need a dozen tough men to ride out in a secret posse. If he doesn't clean them gun hands out, we'll do it for him."

"You think they're wanted?" the deputy asked.

"They damn sure ain't angels."

"How many does he have?"

Dell was watching the street and passing rigs. "We need to find out. You know that old Comanche? Judge Jones?"

"Yeah, what about him?"

"I think he could get us a count and no one would ever know a thing."

"What should we pay him?"

"Give him ten bucks. Tear it in two and tell him that he gets the other half when we know how many gun hands Emerson really has."

"We can try it," Wilbur said. "I'll go ahead and start enlisting the posse, too."

"Do it quietly," Dell warned. "If he has very many, we'll use the Ranger method of getting them out of bed to check their histories out."

Wilbur smiled. "I know how good that works. Anything else stirring?"

"Not unless you heard something. That guard yesterday said someone had burned a haystack up at the Emerson Ranch. Tom never reported it. I wonder what the truth is?"

This drew a smirk. "If I'd thrown a match down and it caught hay on fire, I'd blame someone else, too."

"Exactly what I think. Easy to blame someone else. They also said Tom's other boy broke a leg. Blamed that on his neighbors too."

Wilbur was laughing by then. "I heard was some bronc tossed him off over his head."

"Lots of stories being told. We'll —"

Dell stopped and turned as the front door burst open again.

"Sheriff, you have a wire." The red-faced boy must have run all the way from the Telegraph Office. He had a hand on the doorframe for support while he caught his breath.

Dell traded him a dime for the yellow paper.

Sheriff Dell Hoffman —
Your man Rollo Manus arrested Las Vegas, NM — Being held in local jail for Texas authorities — Thanks for the tip.
— US Deputy Marshal Jim Donaldson

He sat down and wrote a reply.

US Deputy Marshal Jim Donaldson —
Thanks — I will see you get any reward.

— Dell Hoffman, Saddler County
Sheriff Texas

The boy took his tip and the money to send the return message back to the wire office.

Wilbur sent the Comanche out to count the Emerson gunmen aboard his burro, wearing a feather-clad top hat and a bone vest on over his tattered suit coat. Most folks were accustomed to seeing the old man wandering around chanting his old warrior songs and begging food or liquor. He'd made a good lookout for the sheriff's office before — this job should be an easy one for him.

Joel McElroy, the banker from Wayne's Bridge, was there doing business that day. Texas State Banking Examiners had told Dell that they wanted to sell this new man the bank and recover as much of the old bank's outstanding debt to repay the past depositors. He had no objections and had eaten lunch with the man twice when he was in town. McElroy appeared to be an honest man, anxious to fill in the demands for financial services again in the town. Billy

Lee and the other official also agreed — the sooner the better for all concerned.

He made several posters to have a young man put up in store windows. "Our town's head bank robber Rollo Magnus is in Las Vegas, NM jail. Soon to be transported back to Texas on charges. Sheriff Hoffman."

"Be nice to have had a newspaper to print it out in, huh, Wilbur?"

"One will come," the deputy said. "We're growing here."

"With our luck, some fussy woman will come with one and want the saloon closed and all the dogs tied up. And no loud picnics on Sunday."

Wilbur laughed. "We damn sure might get one of those. There ain't no choosing in that deal."

Later in the day, Dell walked home, still amused some about Wilbur's idea about abolitionists starting a newspaper in their town. He'd have to share that with Guinn. She'd find humor in it, too. Heavens, she might even campaign along with them. No, not his Guinn, but some other townswomen might march under a No Drinkers Allowed banner.

Be a short parade, though. Main Street was only two blocks long.

Laughing when he came in to hang up his

hat and gun belt, he told her the story.

She had a good laugh, too. "You sound like you are much better."

"On top of that, Rollo Magnus is in the Las Vegas jail tonight."

"Wonderful!" She clapped her hands together.

"We can celebrate," he said, smiling broadly.

"Hurrah. What else?"

Dell pulled her close. "I'm married to the sweetest woman alive."

"Better let me check on the bread in the oven. It may burn."

Another day and one more dollar, he was walking his life away in good shape and fine company. And the bread didn't get burned, either.

Seventeen

The Comanche came back next morning and showed them seven fingers. Dell replaced his torn money for a whole one. After the Indian left, he paced the jail floors.

"The question at hand," Wilbur said thoughtfully, "is why in the hell do you need that many hired guns to begin with?"

"Well, they damn sure ain't no plain cowboys," Dell answered. "Him and his boys could herd all the cattle they have and not need one puncher."

"And them kind don't work for twenty and beans," Wilbur agreed.

"Obviously, he's keeping them hid. They don't come and join the regulars we see here on the weekends."

"Must go to Kerrville for their sporting. Or somewhere farther out."

"Somewhere, anyway." He didn't like this at all.

"Guess that guard really made it clear he

wasn't no ordinary cowpoke?"

"I thought about him a lot riding back," Dell said. "I had a good hunch he had more, but the number old Comanche brought us is really high."

"Sure did shock me." The deputy rubbed his jaw, deep in thought. "When do we make the raid?"

"Next Monday morning at sunup. They should be road weary and hung over."

"Leave here about midnight?"

"No. Let's meet out at Cloak's Crossing about that time. I want this secret as can be."

Wilbur agreed. "We'll be there."

With the plan in place, Dell went to see Billy Lee. He might need a search warrant to take along. He found his old friend in his office alone working on some paperwork.

"Pull up a chair." The JP took off his reading glasses and shook Dell's hand. "What's going on?"

Dell sat down heavily and took off his hat. "I was checking out this trouble between the Circle H and the Emersons and made a discovery. Tom Emerson has put several pistoleros on his payroll — seven, by my count. One of them guarding the gate stopped me short of the ranch house and turned me back. I ordered Tom to come in and talk to

271

me. When he did, I told him to get rid of the gun hands. He bowed up and refused. I need a search warrant for next Monday for a confidential ranch search to give them shipping orders in person."

"What's he up to?"

"I think he wants to start a range war and run the big outfits out of the country," Dell said. "Of course, it won't happen. They have deeper pockets than he does and I won't tolerate a shooting war down here."

"I agree. I'll get it drawn up and delivered to you."

"Not a word."

"I understand." Billy Lee nodded. "Hey, while we're talking, I heard about the gang ringleader getting picked up. What's his name? Majors?"

"Magnus," he said. "It's good news all right, but I won't relax until they get him to El Paso to face federal charges. He's a slick one."

"I know, but you've damn sure done a job on that bunch I bet they never expected."

"Yeah." He frowned. "Maybe."

"Amy more attempts on your life?"

"Thank God, no." He laughed. "And good thing, too. Guinn'd tan my hide if there were. She's up in arms about all this."

"That's understandable."

"The town gave me a nice new horse. Raised some money for me, too."

"We all appreciate what you get done around here, Dell," his old friend said. "How's your boy?"

"Doing great. Quinn and her sister are having a ball with him."

"You need any backing for this thing with the Emersons, just let me know. I'll be around."

"I appreciate that. We're fine for now, though."

After saying their goodbyes, Dell walked over to Ralph's Saddle and Harness Shop. The bell rang on the door as he entered.

"Leave it open, Dell. I can use some air in here." Ralph was working on building a new saddle on a rawhide-covered tree.

"Looks like you've got plenty of work," Dell said, looking around.

"Business is good." Ralph put down his little hammer. "I have a several saddle orders and at least seven pairs of harness to rebuild. You get any spare time, you can come work here."

"You wouldn't like my patch methods."

Ralph laughed. "That baby boy sure is big in our lives now, huh?"

"He's got the front page, anyhow," Dell agreed. "Say, Ralph. Between you and me, have you heard anything about the hard bunch Tom Emerson hired recently?"

"No. Nothing. Been pretty quiet. How many's he got?"

"Half a dozen."

Ralph whistled. "What's he up to?"

"Wants to start a range war, run off the bigger ranchers."

"Man, no bank here. We don't need that."

"I think that McElroy feller will make the swap with Texas Banking and move in over here," he said. "But I've got no time or space for a damn war."

"That's for sure. I'll keep my ears open."

"Thanks, partner. And if you hear something and can't find me, let Wilbur know. He's working with me to get it smashed before it begins."

He left Ralph and went on to the livery. Rob Perlman threw him a wave from the doorway, where he stood smoking a cigar. "I've got a boy out riding your horse around to get him in condition."

"Good idea. He's stout, but riding him around some more won't hurt him any."

Perlman blew smoke in a thick, blue cloud. "I hear they arrested the ringleader of the gang that robbed the bank."

"They did, but I told Billy Lee I wouldn't be happy until they've got that fox in jail in

El Paso. He's a pretty slick customer." Dell shook his head. "He avoided arrest when we got his hired guns at Mesilla, then me and the Rangers missed him the next morning in El Paso. He had the whole police force down there snowed thinking he was a solid citizen."

"Saw Red Hankins ride through here yesterday." Perlman said.

"I don't reckon I know that name. Who is he?"

"He was in that big Soda Springs scrape a while back. Some big lawyer got him off."

"Another hired gun?"

"What do you mean by 'another?' "

Dell jerked his head toward the rear of the stable. "Let's walk around back by the pens where there ain't no ears, huh?"

"Sure."

When they were out of earshot of anyone else, Dell explained what had happened up on the Emerson ranch and what he thought was going on.

"So you think he's brought in more?" he asked when he was finished.

Perlman shrugged. "Hankins and some other yay-hoo I didn't recognize jogged their horses through here yesterday. They headed east out of town. That's his direction isn't it?"

"Yeah." Dell pounded his fist lightly on a corral post. "He had about half a dozen as of last night — not counting any new ones. I plan to move in Monday morning, break up the party. Most of 'em won't stand a good look at their status on a wanted list."

"Outnumbered and off guard, they should agree to go ahead and ride on," Perlman agreed.

"I don't need the expense or the fuss of arresting and holding them," he said. "Or the chance of another jailbreak because of it."

"That's for damn sure." The liveryman stubbed out the cigar and blew one last cloud of smoke. "Well, you know you need help call on me."

"I think I've got enough help right now. Just keep it all under your hat for me. I don't want word leaking out."

"Don't worry about me. I just hope your plan works. Best way to fight a fire is to piss on it before it gets out of hand."

This drew a chuckle from Dell. "Can't argue with that."

"I wondered why Hankins would come roaming out this way," he said. "More than that, I wondered why he didn't stop at the saloon. He likes to show off, show everyone how big a man he is. Especially with the ladies."

"A damn bully, huh?"

A slow nod. "He sure ain't no blue ribbon citizen to have around."

"We'll try to make his stay a short one."

"Amen. Be careful, Dell. We still need you in office."

"Tom Emerson might not agree with you," Dell said. *Even less by next Monday night.*

His rounds for the morning done, Dell went on to meet Wilbur for lunch down at the Eagle Cafe. On his way back, he stopped at the telegraph office to wire the Fort Worth to Denver railroad conductor. He needed any available boxcar and a whistle stop at Gravel Switch to help move some problems out of his area to the west next Tuesday evening freight special.

Two hours later they sent a reply. It would be handled. If he needed any more information, all he had to do was send another wire. No reply necessary.

Dell smiled and thanked the boy from the Telegraph Office with a dime.

Things were blessedly slow the rest of the week, giving Dell plenty of time to catch up on his paperwork and administration duties. They picked up again on Saturday morning as the weekend shopping crowd made their weekly pilgrimage into town to buy supplies, then hit their peak later that night. Most of the locals were quiet, church-going people, but there were some definite hellraisers and troublemakers among the off-duty hands who lined up at the saloon for drinks and merry-making they couldn't get out on the ranches. Usually it was nothing more than a few drunk and disorderlies — a fight over some dove, or possession of another guy's things. But it didn't take much to spoil the peace and tranquility of a village.

Peace and tranquility were two things much on his mind during this long stretch of downtime — especially the bank robbery. Against all odds, he'd managed to capture the bulk of the gang involved, and yet he still wasn't satisfied with the outcome. The Cody boys — the two who'd started this whole mess — were still at large, as was the dull-witted bank clerk. And while the marshals had finally picked Rollo Magnus up in Las Vegas, he'd heard nothing more from them since the arrest, and that didn't sit right in his craw.

But that wasn't it, exactly. Or, at least, it wasn't all of what was bothering him. Killers were on the loose, and here he was dealing with some pissant rancher trying to start a damn range war.

Late Saturday night after things settled down, Dell brought the new horse home to the house and stabled him in the barn, careful to stay out of sight so as not to send any flags he was fixing to be on the move. The next morning, he and Guinn attended church with the baby. After an extra interminable hour of cooing and crying over his health and cuteness, they'd finally gotten home. Now Teddy was asleep, and they were lying on their bed, fully-dressed, leisurely sipping lips and talking about their future in a nice breeze sweeping the house. It was a nice break from the heat of the past few days.

"You know," he said between kisses. "I keep thinking I should be looking harder for a ranch to get started on."

Guinn laughed. "I think you have some time before Teddy can help you out very much."

"A ranch takes years to build, babe. If we're going to do it, I better find one and get to cutting."

"Have I ever told you how much I appreciate you explaining everything to me?"

"I'm simply glad you listen," he said.

They kissed and hugged each other tightly.

He knew now that he'd never get enough of her. He'd never expected to find a woman so easy to live with and love. She never bitched, never had a headache, or a problem with his job — she was simply there for him. He was one lucky son of a gun, considering all the harping women in the world. Lord knows he dealt with enough of them every day at work.

"I want you to be careful tomorrow, Dell," she told him. "This deal with Tom Emerson might blow up in your face in the morning."

"I'll try to hold my patience in place."

"And your tongue?" She giggled.

He laughed. "Only with him."

"I'll hold you to that." She kissed him, trying not to laugh. "Just come home to me in one piece."

That was exactly how he planned his return — and he'd be glad when the matter was settled.

Next morning, Guinn made him coffee and breakfast at two a.m. Since the baby was asleep, she accompanied him to the barn in her robe. The stars were still out, and the moon's light painted their backyard in stark shades of black and white. She held the lamp for him to thread the latigo strap in the rings to cinch down the saddle. Once finished, he leaned over and kissed her before leading the new horse out of the barn.

Dell caught the reins up close in case the horse felt the urge to buck, but the horse never even humped his back when he slipped into the saddle. Pleased with the animal's progress, he rode out the gate to meet his posse at the edge of town.

He found Wilbur and the others waiting for him at Cloak's Crossing as planned. After counting heads, they mounted up and made for the Emerson Ranch through the cool, predawn gloom. The ride took several hours, and it was still dark when they arrived. Posting two men to cover the ranch house, he took Wilbur and four more to surround the bunkhouse.

With everyone in place, Dell drew his pistol and fired it once into the air. "Rise and shine, boys. This is Sheriff Hoffman. I have an armed posse covering the house and bunkhouse. You're outnumbered and outgunned. File on out here with your hands in the air, or we'll start shooting. *Move.*"

Tom Emerson's voice came out of the darkness from back toward the house. "Gawdamn you, Hoffman! What are you up to?"

"I told you to pay off these gun hands and

send them packing, Tom. I want a wagon and team to haul them up north to the Gravelly Switch, load them in a box car, and send them on their way."

"You can't do that," Emerson protested. "This is a free country."

"Not to start a damn range war, it's not." Dell looked to his deputy. "They all out here Wilbur?"

"We got seven of 'em here, Dell."

"No tricks. Pack your bags and load your tack. My men will unload your guns. You will not reload them in my county. I'm giving you a real break, too. Most lawmen would collect and confiscate them. But you follow my orders, you can keep 'em."

He saw several of the assembled gunmen nod in understanding and appreciation. To be sent somewhere unknown unarmed would be akin to a death sentence for most of them.

Emerson's boy — the one without the broken leg — hitched the team of horses to a wagon, after which the men and their things were loaded and secured. Dell sent a group of four men, led by Wilbur, to escort them to the switch, where they could be loaded in the boxcar he'd arranged for. As the first rosy glints of sunlight crested the eastern horizon, the wagon went rattling north for the switch under the watchful eye of his best man.

Emerson gave him a heaping helping of bluff and bluster while they waited, threatening Dell with all sorts of retribution, starting with a lawsuit.

Finally tiring of the bellyaching, Dell mounted his new horse, and reigned around to face the angry rancher. "Tom, I told you I won't stand for a range war. You try to start things up again, I'll come right back here and put a stop to it. If you make me do that, you and your boys will feel my teeth, I swear to God."

"You ain't telling me —"

"I get off this horse, you won't like what I do to you. You better get on your knees and thank the Lord that you, your wife, and your boys weren't killed in some gun battle brought on by a damn range war that you about started here. Now get out of my sight. *Go!*"

Emerson went.

The outburst did nothing to calm his anger, though. He still felt pent-up enough to shudder from his head to his boots in the stirrup. How hardheaded and just plain dumb could one man be? Dell twisted in his saddle and looked back in the direction of the ranch.

One of the men with him, Rand Carson, was a man his age that owned the Bar Double C. He noticed the look and pushed his horse in closer to Dell. "You know how hard it is to break a dog from eating chickens?"

Dell nodded. "I considered that in this deal. Damn hard. But you know what, Rand? If I have to beat him half to death with an ax handle, I'm going to break him of this. We don't need any feuds round these parts. There's been enough blood spilt in the last few months to last me a lifetime."

"Amen," Carson agreed. "Amen."

Just outside of town, the remaining men of the posse split up and headed for home. These men never expected any pay or reward. They were simply good men, concerned citizens, doing their part for the good of the town, and they made his job one hell of a lot easier.

Smiling in the cool morning air, Dell thanked the good Lord for his good luck and headed for home.

EIGHTEEN

Dell rode on into town to check on the jail and found everything in good order. Paying a boy to take his horse to the livery, he walked home, with no plans other than to spend the day playing with his new son. Instead of going directly into the house, though, he cut across his neighbor's empty lot. He'd left the doors to the barn open when he'd left that morning, and wanted to shut the doors for the night. He'd just grabbed the edge of the door when he heard the unmistakable snort of a horse from inside.

Dell froze.

Why were there horses in his barn? Fear swept through him, an icy ball settling in the pit of his belly. Someone was in his house, waiting for him. Waiting for him with —

Oh, God.

Please, Lord. Please, please don't let any-

285

thing have happened to Guinn or the baby.

Had Magnus hired someone else to kill him? Could Tom Emerson have sent somebody out here to take revenge already? His head swam with visions of the bloody body of the banker's wife, raped and mutilated and thrown across the bed like a piece of trash. Of Clare Willows's body, gutted and filleted like a deer.

His hand dropped to his holster, closing around the wooden grips of his .45.

He had to get hold of himself. He needed to know if anyone was in the barn and how many horses they had hidden there.

Gun in hand, Dell eased around the side of the barn as quietly as he could and slipped in through the back. In the alleyway between him and the door stood three saddled horses, each bearing Mexican saddles with large wooden horns.

He holstered his gun and moved toward the horses. Without thinking, he loosened all the girths so the saddles would fall off if anyone tried to mount them.

A noise came from outside. A commotion, coming this way. Dell moved to the front of the barn to see, but found his view blocked by the house. He turned and scrambled up the ladder to the loft instead, peering out the open second-story door.

He blinked. From down the road, an army of folks were marching toward his house — fifty or sixty people armed with rifles, pistols, pitchforks, and axes. It was a posse, led by none other than Tilly Rawlins, waving them on with a raised six-shooter.

What in the Sam Hill?

As they got closer, he could see others in the crowd. Fred Hanks, Billy Lee — and Angel Cordova.

Now he understood. His gut had been right on the money. Rollo Magnus must have somehow dodged the marshals in Las Vegas and come looking for him. Tilly or Angel must have seen him and raised the alarm.

Son of a bitch!

He had to do something. If Magnus and his cutthroats thought there was no other way out, they wouldn't think twice before butchering Guinn and Teddy.

From the front of the house came a shout, and the sound of a shot. Dell threw himself back down the ladder from the loft and broke for the house, .45 in hand. Up the stairs in three strides, he threw his shoulder against the back door and burst through in a crash of broken wood and shattered glass.

In the kitchen stood a beefy, dark-skinned hombre with a bushy mustache, porkpie hat, and shocked expression on his face. Taken by surprise, the man whirled, grabbing for a pistol on the table between them, but Dell shot him before he'd gotten halfway there. He crumpled to the floor in a heap, clutching a hole in his gut.

From the front room came a scream and the sound of angry voices. Stepping over the felled outlaw, he rushed down the hallway. In the middle of the room, Guinn could be seen rolling across the floor with Rollo Magnus. He was struggling to get his hands around her throat, but she was fighting back, bashing him about the head and eyes every time he got close.

Dell stepped into the room and leveled his six-shooter. "Let my wife go, Rollo. This is between you and me."

"The hell it is!" Magnus screamed. "You took everything I built, Hoffman. Now I'm going to take everything from you and make you watch while I do. Just like your banker friend."

"You make one more —" Dell heard a step behind him. He turned and recoiled as something slammed into the back of his head so hard he saw stars. Fighting the pain, Dell hit the ground and rolled, kicking out one foot to catch his attacker behind the knee. The outlaw fell like a rotten tree, ending up on the floor beside him.

Dell reversed the grip on his revolver and brought the butt end down hard with a sledgehammer blow. The man cried out, then went limp.

Another scream echoed through the room, this one louder than the first. Dell spun, trying to regain his feet. His vision cleared, and he saw Magnus rolling on the ground, grabbing his crotch. Guinn stood over him now, hair streaming around her like red fire.

"How dare you come into my house and lay hands on me and my baby!" She kicked him again, this time in the gut. "Not so tough now, are you, you son of a bitch?"

Magnus howled in pain as Guinn gave him another kick.

"Stop! Please!"

"Did you stop when anyone begged you?" she screamed. Her teeth were clenched and tears were streaming down her face. "Tell me!"

Dell rose and wrapped his wife in his arms. "Guinn, stop. Stop! You've got him. You've got him, sweetheart."

She turned and buried her face in his chest. "Oh, Dell. Oh, God. I thought he was going to kill all of us."

Magnus looked up at them from the floor at their feet, raised himself up on his elbows.

With his free hand, Dell raised his six-shooter and cocked it, aiming it right between his eyes. "You move an inch, Magnus, and I'll gladly put you in the ground."

"Dell? Dell?" The front door swung open and the barrel of a rifle appeared, followed by the face of Fred Hanks. "Dell, you in there?"

"We're good, Fred. We've got it under control."

The town marshal stepped into the room, rifle at the ready, followed by Doc, Billy Lee, and Tilly.

"Are you two okay?" Doc asked.

"We're fine," Dell said. "Guinn, where's the baby?"

Guinn wiped her eyes and sniffled. "In his room, in the crib. That's where the third man was before he hit you."

As if on cue, there came a cry from the other room. Guinn headed that way, and with Hanks now covering Magnus, Dell holstered his revolver and followed. By the time he got there, she had him out of the crib and cradled in her arms, just as he should be — safe and unharmed. He wrapped them both in a hug and sighed.

"Thank God you two are all right."

"They were here to kill us," she whispered.

"I know." He held them tighter. "I found their horses in the barn when I went to close the door. Before I could do anything, I saw the posse coming up the road. They must have seen them ride in here and sounded the alarm."

"We did," came a voice from the door. They looked up. Tilly and Angel stood in the open doorway, looking relieved.

"I'm sorry?" Guinn asked.

"I was in the mercantile getting some things," Tilly said. "Angel come in and told me she'd just seen the man that killed the banker's family ride through. After what happened in El Paso, the only thing we could think of that would bring him back here was — well, killing you."

Angel took up the story. "So we talked to Marshal Hanks, and he rounded up as many people as he could to come help."

Dell chuckled. "Guinn, this is Tilly Rawlins and Angel Cordova."

"It's nice to meet you both," his wife said, still rocking the upset baby. "We owe you so much. I'll never be able to thank you enough."

The two women of the night looked at each other and blushed. They weren't used to such sentiments.

"Hey, Dell?" Billy Lee called in from the

living room. "One of these dogs is dead. What do you want us to do with the other two?"

Dell excused himself as the ladies fawned over Teddy. Back in the parlor, he looked around. Fred Hanks had Magnus and his compatriot face down on the floor and shackled.

"I got 'em all ready, Sheriff," Hanks said. "But I'm afraid the second one had a little accident on your floor."

Sure enough, a slowly-spreading puddle of urine could be seen seeping out from under the second prisoner, trickling toward a nearby throw rug.

Dell shook his head in disgust. "Get 'em out of my house and into the jail where they belong."

Hanks hauled Magnus and "Pee-in-his-pants" to their feet and pushed them on out the door. They were met outside with jeers and shouts from the assembled townspeople.

"Don't hang them yet, folks," Dell shouted after them. "Let the law do that for you."

"Whyn't you deputize a few of us to do it for you, then, Dell?" some wit shouted back, drawing a big laugh.

Dell looked around. Everyone had hustled around raising windows to clear out the gun smoke and the hot Texas wind was doing a good job of it — but not without many teary-eyed faces. Some of the hangers-on had carried the dead *vaquero* out of the kitchen and placed him on the front porch. Someone told him the funeral wagon was on the way to pick up the body. In the meantime, Billy Lee had found a towel to soak up the "wet" bandit's accident in the middle of the floor.

He turned back to the three women and his son. "Well, we stopped a range war today and finally have Rollo Magnus behind bars. I'd call that a good day."

There were hugs all around. Guinn invited Tilly and Angel to eat supper, and they both accepted. Then she handed Dell the baby, and they went with her to the kitchen to prepare it.

Later that night, when he and Guinn were finally alone, he asked her what they'd talked about.

"Normal things," she replied with a knowing smile. "They're both very sweet. They haven't got a grudge one against you, and both told me they felt like you protected them like any other citizen."

Dell chuckled. "Never in my life would I have expected them to lead a posse up here to save you and Teddy."

"Wasn't that something?"

"Tilly least of all. I thought she hated me. But sometimes you don't know who your real friends really are."

"Oh! You never told me how the Emerson deal went."

He waved it away. "We shipped the gunmen out by a freight train like we'd planned. Wilbur should be back by dark. Tom puffed up and called me all sorts of names, but I told him on his life not to try to start any more damn range wars."

"Then it was a good day." She kissed him tenderly. "And we all made it through alive."

"Thank the good Lord," he agreed.

NINETEEN

Things in Thomas City soon simmered down.

After several days of interrogation, Rollo Magnus broke and spilled his entire story, from his original escape after the Ranger raid in Mesilla to how the marshals had missed him in Las Vegas. The truth of the matter was, he'd never even been there. After ducking Dell and the Rangers in El Paso, he'd traveled north, camping out in nearby Scott County to wait for the right chance to get back at the man who'd dismantled his slaving operation. When he'd tired of waiting, he came up with a plan to draw Dell out into the countryside on his own — by raping and murdering Clare Willows in the same brutal fashion as he had the Thompsons months before. The pocketknife Dell had found at the scene belonged to Red Hankins, the *pistolero* Rob Perlman had recognized riding through town a few days before, who they'd arrested with Magnus at the house.

The revelation had shaken Dell. The idea that that poor girl had been tortured and killed as nothing more than bait for him was unforgivable. It was his job to protect the people of his town. Not bring harm down upon them.

Several weeks later, Magnus and Hankins were moved to the San Angelo jail for trial.

Afterward, life returned to normal in his little Texas town. Being sheriff returned to a quieter job again. There were no more range wars, and no more brutal, bloody murders, thank the good Lord. The new bank opened, and gradually the whole place began to get back on its feet.

A pencil-written letter came to him the next spring.

To the Sheriff

Otis Cody is hiding out in Winter County. I knowed them boys from when I was kids. We went to school together. He was always a bully. I am living a better life today than I did back then and don't want to disclose my where abouts to anyone up there nor alert my man to my past. I am sure you understand my concern. He and a Mexikan whore is living on the Letterman Ranch. Good luck getting him.

A friend

"What is it?' Wilbur asked, as Dell stared off at the bare adobe wall in front of his desk.

"Ever hear of any relations to the Codys named Letterman?"

The deputy looked confused. "No, I never heard that name before. Why do you ask?"

"Someone sent me a letter about Otis living with a Mexican woman on their ranch down in Winter County."

"Who?"

Dell held up the paper. "No name on the note. I expect it's a woman, though. She don't want her name involved."

"Winter County? Well that ain't too far away, is it?"

"Not at all. I'd bet these Letterman people are some kin to them and hiding them out of family loyalty."

"It damned sure ain't because he's a likable sort." Wilbur chuckled. "You want me to go ask Hansel Curry if he knows anyone down there?"

"No." He shook his head. "My brother-in-law would be better to answer that. Ralph's been here all his life. If anyone's heard of the connection, it'll be him, and he can keep his mouth shut about it."

"Be nice to finally wrap up this case once and for all."

"You're telling me." Dell folded up the letter and rose. "Hey, you go on ahead and grab lunch off the bar at the saloon and we'll talk more about this later." With Rollo and Hankins gone, the jail was empty. They could get away with both of them being gone. Wilbur agreed, so they locked up and headed out.

Dell walked on down the street to the saddle shop. Redfaced and sweat-soaked, Ralph was making some new driving lines for someone and looked up at Dell's entry like he was grateful to straighten up and set down his leather knife.

"Hey, Dell. What can I do for you today?"

"I got a letter I want to show you. Maybe you can make sense of it."

Ralph held the letter up in the light shining through the side window. When he finished, he nodded. "I'd bet good money I know who wrote this."

"You know her?"

"There was a family lived up on Whitney Creek. The Mosses. They had a passel of kids that went to school with me. Lydia May was one." Ralph rubbed his chin thoughtfully. "She got in trouble a lot. She wasn't more than thirteen when she quit school. We all knew she was carrying someone's baby. I suspected it was one of the Otis boys, but in them days it was all hush-hush. No one talked about it except in whispers. Word was the baby died at birth that next spring and they moved on. A few months back, an old friend of mine, Buck Ridenour, needed a saddle fixed when he came through here, told me he'd seen Lydia May in Edenville. That's in Winter County. She's married to a big rancher down there now, has three nice kids — a shiny looking bunch. I'd bet anything she wrote this."

"I guess as brazen as Otis was, he might have been the sire of that dead baby."

Ralph's lips were pressed together and he nodded before he said, "He was never any fun to be around at school. He may well have been the one did that to her. You going down there after him?"

Dell nodded. "After the Magnus Trial. Don't say a word. You know this Letterman?"

"He married the old man's brother's daughter. Karen, I think her name was. They're older than we are, but she'd be Otis's cousin. Probably why he's there. Them Codys' blood is thicker than cold molasses. You know that."

"Unfortunately," he agreed. "Thanks for the help, Ralph. This note's a real help. If I can catch Otis, he won't get out again."

"You heard any news on where Christopher's at?"

"One more thing to run down," Dell said. "Maybe Otis'll have something to say about him."

"Guinn'll remember Lydia May," Ralph said. "So will Nan. We all went to school together."

"I'll go back to picking up the pieces. Thanks again, buddy."

"Anytime. Kinda nice, ain't it? All we have to do now is go on living."

"That's for sure." Dell shrugged. "I just wish we'd been able to catch them all earlier."

"Oh — wait." Ralph stopped him. "I know it's early, but Nan told me last night she thinks she might be with child."

"That would be great news. You two been married how long?"

Ralph smiled. "Eight years. I sure hope so. Guinn took a long time, too."

"Teddy sure is the deal. I'll act surprised when I hear about it, though."

Dell went on to the saloon to meet Wilbur and eat off the free lunch bar. When they got back to the jail, he filled his deputy in on what Ralph had told him about Otis.

"So we're going to go look for him after the trial in San Angelo? You don't think he'll bolt by then?"

"I figure he feels safe enough to stay there for a while."

Dell spent the rest of the day doing paperwork before walking home. Guinn met him there with a hug.

"You'll never guess who may be pregnant," she gushed.

"Who?"

She squealed happily. "Nan! Can you believe that? After eight years? She's so happy she's dancing!"

"I'll bet Ralph's the same."

"I want to tell you, big man. If you've been trying your damndest to get there for that many years, it was earth shaking for me to learn I had baby in my belly at last."

"Absolutely wonderful. I got good news today, too." He pulled the Cody letter from his vest pocket and handed it over.

Guinn took the note and read it slowly, then went back over it a second time. "This is a real break, isn't it?"

"Oh, yes. Ralph thinks the lady who wrote it is a girl you went to school with."

"Who's that?"

"Lydia May Moss?"

"I haven't heard that name in years," Guinn said. "But I remember her."

"Another one of your classmates came through to get his saddle fixed and told Ralph he saw her down in Edenville with her new husband and a nice family."

"You heard the rest of the story?"

"Yes, he told me what happened to her."

"Good. I'm glad the poor girl found a better way."

"Sounds like she did." He sniffed the air. "Hey, I smell something good in here."

"Oh, dinner's ready. Come on let's eat." She kissed his cheek and then they went to have supper.

He could worry about capturing Otis Cody later.

TWENTY

The district prosecutors shared their concerns with Dell about the high-priced lawyers Rollo Magnus had hired before they moved him to San Angelo — the law firm of Tingle and Davis out of Austin. They had sent several of their young hired guns to San Angelo to set things up before the trial, yelling and making a fuss, demanding all sorts of things the judge had refused. Now the pattern continued after the big fish had arrived for the actual trial. Messrs Tingle and Davis protested and objected so much and so often, Dell's head was spinning by the end of the first day.

But on the other side of the aisle sat Alan Broadhurst, the toughest man in the Texas Judiciary. He was a hellfire and brimstone kind of prosecutor, and when the jury was finally seated he gave them the bloodiest, most brutal descriptions of the Thompson and Willows murders Dell could imagine.

303

He almost believed Broadhurst had seen the bloody mess himself, rather than repeating what Dell had described for him.

When Dell was called to testify, there wasn't much he could add in the way of setting the scene. Broadhurst had already done that. His job was to provide the meat of the case — what clues he'd found, details of his interviews — though not his methods — and how he'd come to the conclusion that Rollo Magnus had been the mastermind of the caper. After he'd finished, Broadhurst called Angel Cordova to the stand.

In the weeks before the trial, Guinn had become fast friends with Angel and Tilly, and Dell knew his wife had helped prepare her for appearance here today. Angel looked like a different woman as she was sworn in. Her accent had faded somewhat. She wore makeup and a pretty teal dress edged with black lace, and her lush black hair was curled and pinned in the most attractive of ways. She answered Broadhurst's questions about Magnus and the bank cashier in a calm, dignified manner, completely unruffled by Rollo's ugly glare from the defendant's table. Dell could see the jury responding to her, and felt a rush of pride for the girl. She'd really come into her own.

She lost none of her composure during the cross-examination, either. Not even when Davis exposed her as nothing more than a prostitute, unworthy of belief as a legal witness. Broadhurst had skipped that part in his direct examination, painting her relationship with the cashier as an affair rather than a transaction. It had little effect, though. Most men accepted women of the night as a normal part of any community, providing a necessary service. By trying to embarrass and shame Angel on the stand, the lawyer had only made her more sympathetic to the jurors and lent that much more weight to her words.

The jury was only out two hours before returning with the expected guilty verdict. Filled with righteous indignation, Rollo's fancy lawyers demanded an appeal, promising to defend the "innocent businessman from El Paso" clear to the Supreme Court. Unimpressed, the judge ordered him hung by month's end. The teenaged Mrs. Magnus and her toddler cried from the benches.

Stepping up to bar, Dell shook hands with Broadhurst and his prosecution team. Rollo Magnus, in handcuffs once again, glared at him from across the way.

"This isn't over, Hoffman," he spat.

Dell chuckled in agreement. "No, it's not,

Rollo. You've still got a couple of weeks left before you swing."

"Just keep looking over your shoulder, lawman. When you least expect it, I'm gonna be there."

"Only if you're a haint, I'd say." He turned to Angel. "You ready to head on home, Angel?"

"Anytime you are, *Señor* Hoffman."

"Let's go." Tipping his hat to Broadhurst, Dell led the way toward the courtroom doors.

"Hoffman!" Magnus's voice called after him. "Remember what I told you. Hoffman. Hoffman!"

He was still yelling when the heavy oak doors closed behind them.

Twenty-One

They drove back to Thomas City in Dell's new buckboard. After spending a night at a hotel in Sweetwater, they arrived at noon the next day.

Word of the verdict had travelled fast, reaching the town well before them by telegram. People were celebrating in the streets. Wilbur met them at the jail with a huge smile plastered across his face. When Dell got home, Guinn was so happy she wanted to dance in the living room. It was a good day. The horrific crime that had devastated the town was almost put to bed.

Almost.

Monday morning, Dell rose early, saddled his horse, and kissed Teddy and Guinn goodbye.

"Be careful," his wife told him as he swung himself up into the saddle. "This is almost over. I don't want to lose you now."

"You won't." He grinned. "That's a promise, Missus Hoffman."

With that, he rode off, headed southwest to find Otis Cody.

Two days later, and with that much growth of beard on his face, Dell sat crouched in a patch of willows alongside a lanky cowboy named Buck Ridenour, Ralph's old friend who had agreed to help him capture Otis.

"You know," Buck said, chewing thoughtfully on a plug of tobacco. "I always wanted to ask Guinn out when I was a teenager, but I was so damn bashful back then I couldn't go through with it."

"Really?" Dell chuckled. "You ain't very bashful now. Takes courage to tell a woman's husband that anytime, I'd think. But especially when he's armed."

Ridenour laughed. "I guess you're right about that."

"She said she remembered you when I told her about you and Ralph meeting up a few months back."

"Some ol' red-faced boy with a stuck tongue tryin to talk to her."

Dell shook his head. "Nah, she had a good impression of you — wait. . . . You hear that?"

"A rider's coming." Ridenour checked his rifle chamber, clicked it shut, and rose to his knees ready to shoot. Dell followed suit.

A moment later, a horseman appeared from behind the trees leading down to the creek. The cleft in the chin and the shock of red hair under the cowboy hat made him unmistakable.

Otis Cody.

"Stop right there, Cody," Dell ordered. "This is Dell Hoffman. Stop or we shoot."

Cody had his gun drawn and his horse turned around with lightning speed, but he'd made the wrong move — there was no way for him to accurately shoot over his shoulder. Two rifles fired together, and the eldest Otis son pitched out of the saddle facedown in the water and didn't move. The horse raced off back the way he'd come.

"Damn," Ridenour breathed. "You warned him, too."

"We did all we could," Dell told him. "At least we saved the state of Texas the cost of hanging him."

"I'd never looked at it that a way." Ridenour smiled and extended a hand. "It was good to meet you, Dell. You tell that great wife of yours the freckle-faced guy who liked her so much in school says howdy."

Dell took the hand and shook it. "I'm sure she'll be pleased to hear that, Buck. But one of us better go catch that horse. We still have to bury the man."

"Being a damn law man is real work, isn't it?"

"This ain't the half of it."

Two days later, Dell rode back home. After a short visit with Guinn and the baby, he sat down to relax for the first time in what seemed like forever. His wife had laid the latest Fort Worth newspaper out in the living room by his chair. On the front page was a banner headline in big, bold letters.

CONVICTED MURDERER SHOT BY RANGERS IN STAND-OFF.

Christopher Cody age 22, a convicted murderer, fugitive, and escapee from Thomas City in Saddler County, was gunned down in the company of two un-identified Mexican nationals in an at-tempted bank robbery in Via Maria, Texas. Word of the attempt had been passed to Ranger Captain Harold Brooks, who dis-patched a company of Rangers to the bank to prevent the robbery.

Cody is the younger brother of Otis Cody, who was recently drowned in a creek after a brief firefight with law enforce-ment from Thomas City.

Dell began laughing.

Guinn peeked in from the kitchen, her eyebrows raised. "What's so funny?"

"Did you read this story in the paper?"

"Yes."

"Otis! It makes it sound like I drowned him."

"Oh, who cares?" She threw her arms up, and then landed in his lap where they both laughed. "It's over, Dell. All of it. And I have you back in one piece."

What the hell, Dell thought. She was right. It was all over but the shouting, and none of that mattered, anyway. What really counted was this — his wife, their son, and a badge worth polishing.

ABOUT THE AUTHOR

Dusty Richards grew up riding horses and watching his western heroes on the big screen. He even wrote book reports for his classmates, making up westerns since English teachers didn't read that kind of book. But his mother didn't want him to be a cowboy, so he went to college, then worked for Tyson Foods and auctioned cattle when he wasn't an anchor on television.

But his lifelong dream was to write the novels he loved. He sat on the stoop of Zane Grey's cabin and promised that he'd get published. And in 1992, his first book, *Noble's Way,* hit the shelves. Since then, he's had 151 more come out.

If he can steal some time, he also likes to fish for trout on the White River.

Facebook: westernauthordustyrichards
www.dustyrichardslegacy.com

The employees of Thorndike Press hope you have enjoyed this Large Print book. All our Thorndike, Wheeler, and Kennebec Large Print titles are designed for easy reading, and all our books are made to last. Other Thorndike Press Large Print books are available at your library, through selected bookstores, or directly from us.

For information about titles, please call:
   (800) 223-1244

or visit our website at:
   gale.com/thorndike

To share your comments, please write:
   Publisher
   Thorndike Press
   10 Water St., Suite 310
   Waterville, ME 04901